All of
a l

Laura, who could only looking at Danny's horrible features, had no idea what had just happened. All she knew was that Danny wasn't attacking her anymore.

Then he just started to fall apart—literally. His face started to flake and collapse, his hair and clothes and leather jacket all became a fine powder, and then—

—then nothing. Just dust on the Waverly Place sidewalk.

Now the girl was standing in front of Laura, holding a piece of wood in her hand. Behind her, Jackson was on the sidewalk, leaning up against a fire hydrant, shaking his head.

"Th-thank you," Laura managed to blurt out. Tears were streaming down her cheeks.

The girl just smiled, then turned and ran toward Jackson, the piece of wood raised up. Jackson managed to kick her in the stomach before she could get too close, but then she grabbed his ankle with her left hand and yanked him closer to her, pulling him away from the hydrant, his head hitting the sidewalk with what Laura thought was a pretty hollow crack.

With her right hand, the girl plunged the piece of wood into Jackson's chest.

He turned into dust too.

It was the freakiest thing Laura had ever seen.

Buffy the Vampire Slayer™

Buffy the Vampire Slayer
 (movie tie-in)
The Harvest
Halloween Rain
Coyote Moon
Night of the Living Rerun
Blooded
Visitors
Unnatural Selection
The Power of Persuasion
Deep Water
Here Be Monsters
Ghoul Trouble
Doomsday Deck
Sweet Sixteen
Crossings
Little Things

The Angel Chronicles, Vol. 1
The Angel Chronicles, Vol. 2
The Angel Chronicles, Vol. 3
The Xander Years, Vol. 1
The Xander Years, Vol. 2
The Willow Files, Vol. 1
The Willow Files, Vol. 2
How I Survived My Summer Vacation,
 Vol. 1
The Cordelia Collection, Vol. 1
The Faith Trials, Vol. 1
The Journals of Rupert Giles, Vol. 1
Tales of the Slayer, Vol. 1
Tales of the Slayer, Vol. 2
Tales of the Slayer, Vol. 3
Tales of the Slayer, Vol. 4

The Postcards
The Essential Angel Posterbook
The Sunnydale High Yearbook
Pop Quiz: Buffy the Vampire Slayer
The Monster Book
The Script Book, Season One, Vol. 1
The Script Book, Season One, Vol. 2
The Script Book, Season Two, Vol. 1
The Script Book, Season Two, Vol. 2
The Script Book, Season Two, Vol. 3
The Script Book, Season Two, Vol. 4
The Script Book, Season Three, Vol. 1
The Script Book, Season Three, Vol. 2
The Musical Script Book: Once More, With Feeling
The Watcher's Guide, Vol. 1: The Official Companion to the Hit Show
The Watcher's Guide, Vol. 2: The Official Companion to the Hit Show
The Watcher's Guide, Vol. 3: The Official Companion to the Hit Show

The Lost Slayer serial novel
 Part 1: Prophecies
 Part 2: Dark Times
 Part 3: King of the Dead
 Part 4: Original Sins
 Omnibus Edition
Child of the Hunt
Return to Chaos
The Gatekeeper Trilogy
 Book 1: Out of the Madhouse
 Book 2: Ghost Roads
 Book 3: Sons of Entropy
Obsidian Fate
Immortal
Sins of the Father
Resurrecting Ravana
Prime Evil
The Evil That Men Do
Paleo
Spike and Dru: Pretty Maids
 All in a Row
Revenant
The Book of Fours
Tempted Champions
Oz: Into the Wild
The Wisdom of War
These Our Actors
Blood and Fog
Chosen
Chaos Bleeds
Mortal Fear
Apocalypse Memories
Wicked Willow Trilogy
 The Darkening
 Shattered Twilight
 Broken Sunrise
Stake Your Destiny
 The Suicide King
 Keep Me in Mind
 Colony
 Night Terrors
Queen of the Slayers
Spark and Burn
Afterimage
Carnival of Souls
Go Ask Malice: A Slayer's Diary
Blackout

Available from POCKET BOOKS

Blackout

Keith R. A. DeCandido

**An original novel based on the hit television series
created by Joss Whedon**

POCKET
BOOKS

LONDON • SYDNEY • NEW YORK • TORONTO

This book is a work of fiction. Any references to historical events, real people, or real locales are used fictitiously. Other names, characters, places, and incidents are the product of the author's imagination, and any resemblance to actual events or locales or persons, living or dead, is entirely coincidental.

POCKET BOOKS
An imprint of Simon & Schuster Ltd.
Africa House, 64–78 Kingsway, London WC2B 6AH
™ & © 2006 Twentieth Century Fox Film Corporation. All rights reserved.
All rights reserved, including the right of reproduction in whole or in part in any form. Originally published by Simon Spotlight Entertainment, an imprint of Simon & Schuster, Inc, NY. "BUFFY THE VAMPIRE SLAYER" is a trademark of Twentieth Century Fox Film Corporation, registered in the U.S. Patent and Trademark Office.
POCKET BOOKS and related logo are trademarks of Simon & Schuster Ltd.
Printed and bound in Great Britain by
Cox & Wyman Ltd, Reading, Berks
First Edition 10 9 8 7 6 5 4 3 2 1
ISBN-13: 978-1-4165-2636-0
ISBN-10: 1-4165-2636-6
A CIP catalogue record for this book is available from the British Library

**Dedicated to the fond memory of
Gordon Parks—photographer, author,
composer, and filmmaker, the latter including
the seminal film *Shaft*.**

Here's to a bad mother—

(Shut yo' mouth!)

But I'm just talkin' 'bout Gordon!

Acknowledgments

First of all, I must thank Doug Petrie, who gave us Nikki Wood in the fifth-season *Buffy* episode "Fool for Love," and without whose efforts this book would be much shorter. Also thanks to David Fury and Drew Goddard, who fleshed Nikki out in the seventh-season episode "Lies My Parents Told Me." Scenes from those two episodes are incorporated into the narrative that follows, and I owe a large debt to all three writers for giving me something to work with. I hope that what follows does justice to what they created.

Secondly, I must thank my wonderful editor Beth Bracken, who shepherded this book through magnificently and kept me on track when I might've gotten derailed. (Oooh, *beat* that subway metaphor into the ground!) Gratitude also to Debbie Olshan at Fox, who nipped some authorial infelicities in the bud, and to Cara Bedick and Terra Chalberg.

Thirdly, thanks to the two women who gave Nikki life on screen, April Wheedon-Washington and K. D. Aubert, as well as Damani Roberts and D. B. Woodside (the child and adult iterations of Robin Wood, respectively), Juliet Landau (Drusilla), Sarah Michelle Gellar (Buffy), Roy Dotrice (Roger Wyndham-Pryce), and most especially the incomparable James Marsters (Spike); and also to the writers of the numerous *Buffy* and *Angel* episodes that provided background material that helped solidify this book in the complex and wonderful universe those two shows gave us.

Fourthly, gratitude to various reference sources and inspirations: *Buffy the Vampire Slayer: The Watchers Guide*, Volumes 1–3; CBGB.com and the DVD *Dead Boys at CBGB 1977*; the movies *Shaft*, *Shaft's Big Score!*, *Superfly*, *Cleopatra Jones*, *Foxy Brown*, *Hell Up in Harlem*, *Across 110th Street*, *The Black Godfather*, and so many other contemporary flicks; the various comic books published by Marvel starring Luke Cage, aka Power Man, aka Hero for Hire; the TV shows *Barney Miller*, *Good Times*, and *What's Happening!!*; the book *Down 42nd Street: Sex, Money, Culture, and Politics at the Crossroads of the World* by Marc Eliot; the good folks in the Microforms Room at the New York Public Library, who provided me with various summer 1977 newspapers; and the work of the reporters who wrote for those newspapers, in particular Jimmy Breslin's columns on the Son of Sam and Pete

Hamill's account of the night of the 1977 blackout.

Also: Lucienne Diver (my wonderful agent), Lisa Clancy (my editor on *The Watchers Guide,* Volume 1 and *The Xander Years,* Volume 1, my previous forays into *Buffy* books), Christopher Golden, Nancy Holder, Laura Anne Gilman, Lesley McBain, Terri Osborne, the Forebearance (especially the Mom, GraceAnne Andreassi DeCandido), Diana G. Gallagher, Jennifer Crawford, Michael A. Burstein, Jac Fry, *Kyoshi* Paul and everyone else at the dojo, and the staff of the Delacorte Theater, who handled it so well when the blackout of 1977 hit in the middle of the production of *Threepenny Opera* (starring Raul Julia) that my parents and I were attending.

Oh, and I'm told some person named Joss somebody had something to do with this whole thing, so I guess I should thank him, too. No, no; I kid—thanks to Joss Whedon, who gave us such a rich and glorious world to play in.

Blackout

Prologue

Sunnydale, California
January 22, 2002
9:30 p.m.

Spike was looking forward to a pleasant evening. The grocery store had restocked the Weetabix shelf, giving Spike the opportunity to clean it out again; the butcher had plenty of blood; and the little trick with the tree branch in the Blockbuster returns bin had nabbed him a videotape of *Henry V*—Branagh's version, thankfully, not Olivier's. Spike had never been able to stand Olivier. *Pompous wanker, and made it all too pretty.* Branagh's battle sequences felt more real to Spike—who'd participated in plenty of massacres in his time and knew just how messy they were—and the dialogue was more natural, like people talking, instead of that bloody awful declaiming that Olivier and his lads did.

Now Spike walked through the cemetery toward his crypt, in anticipation of a quiet night of blood, Weetabix, and Shakespeare.

Bollocks, he thought as he approached the stone edifice he'd taken as his home. *Is this what it's come to, then? Looking forward to an evening of sitting in front of the telly? I'm turning bloody middle class, I am.*

He had little choice. The chip the Initiative had put in him two years ago had rendered him incapable of harming humans, forcing him to depend on animals, hospitals, or what he could obtain from butchers for his necessary sustenance. He'd stopped with the hospitals of late, however—a promise to Buffy—and stuck with what he could obtain legitimately.

Legitimately. The very word brought him out in a rash. And yet, who was the one who was helping Buffy and Giles and Willow and the rest of them against Glory this past May? Worse, doing it to save a little girl?

Not just a little girl. Dawnie. Little Bit's an innocent in all this, doesn't deserve to be killed.

Yeah, some bloody demon you've turned out to be. Since when do you give a toss about the innocent?

Since she's the sister of the woman you're in love with. Since you promised that woman to protect Dawn at all costs.

And isn't that a kick in the teeth?

Then Spike picked up the scent. A fellow vampire. He smiled. *A scrap's always good to get the old blood flowing.*

"*Damn*, when I heard tell *this* was your pad, I thought they was jivin' me, but there you are."

Spike whirled around to see the vampire. He was dark-skinned—what had been variously referred to in his lifetime as abo, Negro, colored, Afro-American, black, and African-American—and dressed in what Buffy might refer to as "early high pimp." The vamp wore a purple brimmed hat that barely covered an Afro of a size Spike hadn't seen in twenty years at least; a matching purple silk shirt with a massive collar, unbuttoned halfway down the chest and revealing several gold chains; and corduroy pants that flared at the bottom.

The face on the vampire was familiar. "I know you."

"Yeah, you do. Been twenty-five years. 'Course, last time we met, was somebody else wearin' that coat."

Between the clothes and that comment, it clicked into place for Spike. "You were one of Reet's boys, yeah?"

"Leroy—Leroy Hawkins."

Spike nodded and gently set down his grocery bags. He didn't want to risk the Weetabix box getting bruised in the fight. "Didn't I kill you?"

"Damn, honky, I'm 'bout the only one you and that crazy bitch *didn't* kill. You still hangin' with her?"

"We split." Spike didn't provide any more information than that. For one thing, his relationship with Drusilla was none of Leroy's business. For another, the vamp would be dust in two minutes. No sense wasting time.

"Good move, m'man. That lady was *bad* news. After what she did to Reet . . ." Leroy shook his head, the feather in the brim of his purple hat shaking in the light breeze that wafted through the Sunnydale night. "I see you got ridda that punk jive you was wearin'."

"Yeah, well, it was all the rage—then. I try to change with the times. I'd recommend you try it, but you won't be around that long."

"Say *what*? What you talkin' 'bout, man?"

Spike blinked. "You're not here to take revenge?"

Leroy threw his head back and laughed, causing the gold chains to jangle and almost dislodging his hat from its perch atop his Afro. "You crazy? What the hell I want revenge for? Thanks to you, I was *set*. After what you and that lady did, the rackets was *mine*. The Big Apple was ripe for the biting—'specially since you took out the Slayer."

"So if it was so 'ripe,' why are you here?"

Leroy shrugged. "Core got rotten. New York ain't what it used to be, know what I'm sayin'? So I got while the gettin' was good. Worked my way out West, found my way here. Naw, man, I'm here to *thank* you. Heard tell there's a bar in this dump, caters to our kind. If you want, I'll buy you a drink."

Bending over to pick up his groceries, and not even bothering to hide the disappointment in his voice, Spike said, "No, thank you. I'm not exactly welcome there." He'd allied himself with the Slayer, after all, and that made him persona non grata in Willy's bar. He went into the crypt.

Leroy followed him in. "Well, at least tell me

where the good killin' spots are. I figured now's the best time to be in Sunnydale—Hellmouth and all." He looked around. "Sheeee-oot, you call *this* a pad?"

"No, I call it a crypt. The rent's free, the TV works, and I get left alone. Best of all, I don't get a lot of visitors. You might take that hint."

Not doing so, Leroy stepped off the concrete of the doorway into the dirt of the crypt floor. "If I can't get you a drink, tell me what I can do. Man, I *owe* you."

Spike couldn't believe what he was hearing. "Look, mate, the only reason you're still basking in the glory of unlife is because I somehow missed killing you back in the day. Total accident, yeah? Complete oversight on my part, one I'd be more than happy to rectify, if you catch my drift."

"Man, I ain't carin' about the why, I'm carin' about the results. Now you did me a solid, and I wanna pay you back."

"Leaving might be a fine start." Spike set the grocery bag down next to his easy chair and tried to remember where he'd put that stake.

"Come *on*, man, you were the baddest cat on the block! Don't tell me there ain't nothin' I can do for you. Especially *now*. I heard tell the Slayer was dead—got replaced by a robot or somethin' after she got iced by some goddess bitch. That means Sunnydale's open season, am I right?"

A familiar voice sounded from behind Leroy. "Not quite."

Looking past Leroy to the door to the crypt—which the vampire had left open, the wanker—Spike saw the familiar, diminutive form of the Slayer framed by the doorway, moonlight shimmering on her blond hair.

Chuckling, Spike said, "It's getting so a man can't have a quiet evening in this town, can he?"

Leroy turned around to face the new arrival. "Who the hell're you, chickie?"

Buffy Summers smiled. "I'm the Slayer."

"But you're dead."

She shrugged and pulled out a stake. "I got better."

Chapter One

New York City
July 6, 1977
4:50 a.m.

Laura McCarthy cursed John and everything he stood for.

The predawn breeze cut through the thin silk fabric of Laura's dress and set the litter on the sidewalk into a whirl. The paper spinning made a sound like autumn leaves being stepped on, echoing on the streets. This late at night—or early in the morning, depending on how you looked at it—was one of those rare occasions when the island of Manhattan was quiet. It was after the bars and discos finally closed, and before people were getting up to face the new day. The sun hadn't come up yet, and wouldn't for another hour or so.

She never even got John's last name. Not that she cared what it was, really, unless she wanted to send the big jerk a letter bomb.

It had seemed like a good idea at the time. Freddie had broken up with her at Cissy's Fourth of July party. Laura had decided to show him what a real woman could do, so she had put on her best outfit and had gone to the No-Name Bar, fully intending to go home with someone better looking than Freddie.

As she turned the corner onto Sixth Avenue, goose pimples came up on her flesh as the wind intensified, no longer blocked by the buildings on West 3rd. It had been a long, hot, humid summer so far, but it was still cold without the sun up, especially when you had only thin silk to protect you, and not a whole lot of that. She hadn't brought any money with her—a fine-looking chick like herself could depend on men to buy her drinks—and all her tokens must've fallen out of her purse. So she had to walk, even though that Son of Sam freak was still on the loose. Been going on a year now, and the cops had no idea who it was killing people—mostly girls—with a .44 caliber gun. He'd sent letters to the cops and the newspapers and everything, but nobody really knew who he was.

Everybody knew, though, that they probably shouldn't be walking around alone this late at night.

But John hadn't given her much choice. Oh, he had been one smooth-talking man in the bar when the drinks had been flowing. He had come over with his big arms and his deep voice and his tight shirt and his hip sideburns and his thick mustache and told her how pretty she was, and she had eaten it all up as fast as she had drunk the Manhattans he'd bought her.

Her ankle twisted on a crack in the pavement, and she stumbled, trying to recover her footing on the high heels she'd worn. *Why do we wear this stuff?* She knew there was really no logical answer. It was just what you were *supposed* to wear with nice dresses. Still, she kept them on, since she for damn sure wasn't going barefoot. That might be all right for those hippie chicks, but Laura knew just how dirty a New York sidewalk was, and she was keeping her shoes, no matter how uncomfortable, between that filth and her feet.

By the time Laura had had her fifth Manhattan—or maybe it was her sixth—she had been willing to do whatever John wanted, and what he had wanted to do was her. She had eagerly gone with him back to his pad. But after he was done, he had kicked her out. No breakfast, no offer to call her a cab, nothing, he had just said, "Thanks, baby. You were great. But you gotta go. Got *things* to do."

Laura didn't know what kind of *things* anybody had to do at four thirty in the morning, but John had to do them, and he couldn't do them with her there, apparently. So off she went.

It wasn't until she had arrived at the subway station that she had realized she had no tokens. She could have sworn she had some in her purse, but they might've fallen out in John's pad. Or in the No-Name. Or maybe she ran out, she could never keep track of the damn things. She didn't have any cash to buy more tokens, and the banks wouldn't be open for hours.

So she walked.

A Checker Cab went zooming up Sixth, honking its horn at her as she crossed against the light, but not actually stopping. Laura ignored it, simply putting one foot in front of the other on the uncomfortable heels, knowing she'd be home soon. She just had to make it to Waverly and her own apartment, and everything'd be okay. Thank God she had the morning off. They'd put her on the four-to-midnight shift this week, so she could get some sleep tonight—or this morning, or whatever. She just hoped that her roommates were asleep, or had found their own men to go home with. Right now, Laura did not want to deal with people.

"Fine-lookin' chick like you shouldn't be out by yourself, ain't that right, Jackson?"

"That's right, Danny—ain't *safe*."

Laura almost jumped out of her skin at the voices. She hadn't heard them approaching her, hadn't seen them, nothing.

"Yeah," said Danny, who was tall, had a receding hairline, and wore a leather jacket. "See, there's all *kinds* of freaks on the streets this time o' night."

"That's right," Jackson, the shorter one with the thick beard, glasses, and denim jacket said. "A girl might get *hurt*."

Oh, no, it's the Son of Sam! Any minute now, one of them's gonna pull his gun out of that coat!

Laura was about to scream, but Danny moved incredibly fast and covered her mouth with a cold and clammy hand. "Ah, ah, ah. None o' that. We like it quiet." His hot breath smelled like something had died in his mouth.

Then his face changed.

His forehead seemed to get bigger and thicker, his eyebrows disappeared completely, and the bridge of his nose got wider. Eyes that had been brown became sort of greenish and watery.

And his mouth was now filled with huge fangs—which went straight for Laura's throat.

Laura's scream was muffled by Danny's cold hand on her mouth, but she yelled as loudly as she could anyhow. *The cops got it all wrong, the Son of Sam is* two *people, and they're crazy freaks, and oh God, I'm gonna die!*

Suddenly Laura found herself being yanked forward. She stumbled to the pavement, Danny's hand no longer on her mouth, his dead breath no longer right in her face. She looked up to see Danny being pulled up and getting punched by a dark blur. Laura couldn't make out what the figure looked like, except whoever it was had an Afro, wore a big black cape, and moved like Bruce Lee.

The guy's moves were *amazing*. Laura, still prone on the pavement, found herself entranced. First he dodged a punch, grabbed Danny's wrist as he dodged, and pulled him close enough to elbow Danny in the face. As he stumbled backward, the guy in the cape got Danny in the stomach with the other elbow. Afro-guy was a whirlwind, his cape flapping in the breeze, and Danny couldn't land a single punch.

Then Danny got kicked three times in a row, once

in the stomach, once in the chest, and once in the head, without Afro-guy once putting his foot down. That kick to the head sent Danny flying back into the garbage cans in front of Laura's building with a loud clatter. She had gotten a good look at the guy's feet when he made those kicks, and he was wearing platform shoes.

When the guy turned to face Jackson, Laura gasped, because it *wasn't* a man wearing platforms. The streetlight now showed the face clearly, and that was *definitely* a chick. It wasn't a cape, either, it was a leather coat, covering a brown turtleneck (why the hell would anyone wear a turtleneck in *July*?) and bell-bottoms.

Laura couldn't believe it. *Outta sight! Where'd a girl learn moves like that? And where do I sign up?* Laura had never considered herself a women's libber, but after the way Freddie and John had treated her, and seeing this girl in action, she was ready to vote yes on the Equal Rights Amendment right here and now.

Jackson's face had changed the same way, and now he made a weird snarling noise as he jumped for the girl.

She jumped out of the way at the last second, blocking the punch with her left arm, then punching him in the stomach, then knocking him down to the pavement with her arms and legs, moving so fast Laura wasn't even sure how she did it.

After the girl punched Jackson in the face, Laura heard the metallic rattle of the garbage cans. She was about to shout a warning to the girl, but it turned out not to be necessary. Before Laura even had a chance to open her mouth, the girl had stepped and kicked Danny right back into the cans.

"You ain't dustin' us, bitch!" Jackson said as he got to his feet, blood spilling from a cut on his cheek.

The girl just smiled.

Jackson and the girl traded punches, neither one actually landing—no, wait, Jackson got her once, but she just came back with a kick he didn't see coming. Neither did Laura—that bad coat she was wearing made it hard to see her legs. Laura wondered if that was why she wore it, or if it was just to look supercool. *Maybe both*.

Then Danny got up again and jumped her also. Laura was surprised they hadn't done that sooner—made more sense for two of them to attack than one at a time. The girl managed to hold them both off, but they were starting to push her toward the fence in front of Laura's building.

Normally, Laura would have taken this opportunity to run away. She didn't want to get into a fight, and she tried to stay away from trouble. But there were two problems. One, she had nowhere to run *to*—they were fighting *right* in front of her apartment building, and the three of them were between her and the front door. Two, this girl, whoever she was, had just jumped in to help Laura without even knowing who she was, risking her life. Laura had never had a violent thought in her life, but right now, seeing this girl beating up on the two freaks, she suddenly wanted to help the girl out.

This is nuts, Laura thought as she scrambled over to the garbage cans.

A voice yelled down from above. "Keep it down, willya? There's people tryin'a *sleep* here!"

Not letting herself think about how stupid this was, Laura grabbed one of the metal lids and hit Danny on the head with it.

The lid dented, and the vibration shot through her arm so hard she dropped it onto the pavement.

Danny turned around and snarled at her. "Oh, you're gonna be sorry you did that, little girl."

Sweat poured out of Laura's forehead. *Oh God, all I did was make him mad. What the hell was I thinking?*

Baring his fangs, Danny advanced on Laura. She couldn't make herself move her feet—hell, she couldn't make herself *breathe.* Her heart was going a mile a minute. The Son of Sam was gonna kill her. She'd be another victim, just like Donna Lauria and all the others, just some story in the paper. . . .

But why hasn't he taken out his gun yet?

All of a sudden, Danny tensed up, a look of shock on his face. Laura, who couldn't make her head move and was only looking at Danny's horrible features, had no idea what had just happened. All she knew was that Danny wasn't attacking her anymore.

Then he just started to fall apart—literally. His face started to flake and collapse, his hair and clothes and leather jacket all became a fine powder, and then—

—then nothing. Just dust on the Waverly Place sidewalk.

Now the girl was standing in front of Laura, holding a piece of wood in her hand. Behind her, Jackson was on the sidewalk, leaning up against a fire hydrant, shaking his head.

"Th-thank you," Laura managed to blurt out. Tears were streaming down her cheeks.

The girl just smiled, then turned and ran toward Jackson, the piece of wood raised up. Jackson managed to kick her in the stomach before she could get too close, but then she grabbed his ankle with her left hand and yanked him closer to her, pulling him away from the hydrant, his head hitting the sidewalk with what Laura thought was a pretty hollow crack.

With her right hand, the girl plunged the piece of wood into Jackson's chest.

He turned into dust too.

It was the freakiest thing Laura had ever seen.

The girl walked over to Laura, her coat whooshing behind her. She looked like Pam Grier or Tamara Dobson, only cooler. Cleopatra Jones didn't have a *thing* on this chick.

Laura couldn't believe it. This girl had just been in a major fight, and her makeup wasn't even mussed. Not even a bruise or nothing. Before he got arrested, Laura's daddy would hit Laura, and she'd be bloody and bruised all over her face, and her daddy hit her a lot fewer times than this girl got hit by Danny and Jackson.

As for Laura, her silk dress was ruined, she'd broken three nails, and she had scratches on her arms and legs from when she fell to the pavement. But this girl's coat wasn't even out of place.

Somehow, Laura managed to make her lips move. "What—what *were* those guys? Not Son of Sam?"

For the first time, the girl spoke. "No, sugar, they ain't got nothin' to do with that cat. Don't worry, they're gone and they ain't never comin' back, you dig?"

Given that they'd been turned into dust, Laura could believe that. Now what Jackson had said about her not dusting them made sense. But she still didn't get it. "Who—who are you?"

She smiled. "Just call me the Vampire Slayer, baby."

Chapter Two

New York City
July 6, 1977
5:35 a.m.

The sun was just starting to peek over the skyline when Nikki Wood left the apartment on Waverly Place and headed to the West 4th Street station to catch the A train back home. Once the day started, her work was done—vamps didn't do sunlight, which meant Nikki the Vampire Slayer was free to call it a night.

It had been a slow night until she found those two creeps attacking that chick on Waverly. Nikki didn't always stop random muggings—if she started on wholesale crime fighting in this town, it'd become a full-time job, and she already had a mission—but the lack of undead activity meant she was willing to go out of bounds for once and stop some poor girl from getting herself robbed or worse. And then it turned out they were vampires anyhow, so it was all cool.

Summer was always slower, because of the longer days, though there were other creatures that made up for it. Last full moon she'd had to keep an eye on a pack of werewolves that were roaming around Prospect Park in Brooklyn and keep them out of trouble, and then last week there was a weird portal that some kids with a musty old book and too much time on their hands opened in Van Cortlandt Park in the Bronx.

After Nikki dusted those two bloodsuckers, the girl thanked her and told her it would've been a crappy ending to a crappy night after what happened with that John turkey at the No-Name Bar, Nikki then felt the need to give a lecture. She hated when Crowley gave lectures like that, but Nikki had learned the hard way to be careful of men who talked a good game in a bar.

Once she was sure the girl was okay, Nikki took her leave, making sure not to give out a name, even though she was asked. As far as anyone was concerned, she was just the Slayer. If that girl hadn't been such a mess, or if it hadn't been so late at night, Nikki wouldn't have stuck around, but there weren't any other people in sight—just that one jackass who'd yelled for them to keep it down—and it wasn't like the fuzz would be any help if she called them. There was no evidence of the attack, so the cops would just think Nikki and the girl were crazy—just like they had when

Nikki's grandmother was killed by a vampire.

Nikki didn't have much use for the fuzz.

So Nikki took care of the girl for a bit before heading home.

She went down the stairs of the IND train entrance on West 3rd and Sixth. Reaching into her coat, she felt around the change that had collected in the deep pyramid-shaped bottom of the right pocket until she felt a coin with the Y shape carved out of the center. Dropping the token into the slot, she pushed the large wooden turnstile, which rumbled as it rotated to allow her ingress to the subway station. It'd take ages for the A train to show up, but Nikki had been running across rooftops and through side streets on platform shoes all night. She wanted to sit, and being able to do so was worth the wait. Crowley and Robin would likely still be asleep when she got home anyhow.

Luck, however, was with her tonight—the A showed up as soon as she made it to the platform. Only a few winos and some kids were on the graffiti-covered train, and they gave Nikki a wide berth as she sat in the two-seater by the side door. It was hot as hell on the train, even with all the windows open, but Nikki kept her coat on and didn't regret the choice of a turtleneck. When you spent your nights hunting bloodsuckers, it was best to keep your neck covered.

As for the coat—hell, baby, that was her *look*. You didn't mess with the *look*. Besides, she used the coat to cover her moves, like Batman did with his cape in the comics. In fact, that was how she saw herself: as

Cleopatra Jones and Batman, all rolled up in one cool package.

This late, the A train was running local, so it made the full three stops before reaching 42nd Street instead of the two it usually made before pulling into the station below the Port Authority. Her coat sweeping behind her, Nikki ran up the stairs to 42nd Street and the grime of Times Square.

Halfway down 42nd was the Gem Theater, one of a dozen crappy movie theaters in the square. This one distinguished itself from the others in that it showed old Westerns twenty-four hours a day instead of skin flicks, mainly because Olaf Manguson, the theater's owner, could get them cheap. The marquee listed two movies: *My Darling Clementine* and *Rio Bravo*, which were likely alternating. Olaf never did double features, preferring to charge one admission per film.

There was a small two-room apartment behind the projection room, which had been given to Nikki to live in rent-free ever since she saved the life of Olaf's nephew A.J., the theater's manager, by dusting a vampire three and a half years ago.

Marty, the insomniac old man who had the overnight shift in the ticket booth, greeted her as she approached the theater entrance. "Mornin', Nikki. Kill any Commies?"

Nikki smiled. "Not tonight, Marty. Just a coupla vampires."

"Dang. Need to get ridda Commies. S'what we did back in double-ya double-ya two, y'know." Marty frowned. "Wait, that was the Nazis. Korea was the

Commies." Marty had served two tours in the U.S. Marines. He kept his old service revolver handy in the ticket booth, which had been a surprise to many a would-be late-night robber who thought the old man would be easy pickings.

"That ain't the job, sugar. Job's killin' vampires." Marty had been present when Nikki staked the vampire whose death led to her place of residence—and had been frustrated by the uselessness of his revolver against the creature determined to suck A.J.'s blood. It also meant he knew exactly how Nikki spent her nights.

Marty looked thoughtful. "Maybe you could kill vampire Commies?"

"I'll work on it, Marty," Nikki said with a laugh as she went into the theater. A.J. Manguson, tall and skinny with long, straight blond hair, was behind the popcorn counter, trying to keep himself awake. Nikki was surprised to see him standing there, since Leo usually took the overnight at the popcorn counter while A.J. slept. "What's happenin', Ayj? Where's Leo?"

"His wife's sick, so he's gotta take the kids to school this morning. I let him go early."

Nikki nodded. "Quiet night?"

"Yeah, just the usual loonies who can't live without a John Wayne flick at four in the morning. So you catch the Son of Sam yet?"

Laughing, Nikki shook her head. "I'm the *Vampire* Slayer, Ayj. I got a mission, and it don't mean stoppin' no freaks." She realized what she'd said and added quickly, "Not *those* kinda freaks, anyhow. Let the fuzz handle that."

A.J. snorted. "Yeah, 'cause they're doing *such* a good job right now. Been almost a year, and they haven't got a clue."

She moved toward the back staircase that led to the projection room and her pad. "Well, I'm done for the night, sugar. Gonna catch me some z's."

"Right on, Nik. G'night."

Slowly Nikki trudged up the narrow, uneven staircase, the warped old wood creaking each time her platforms came down on them.

At the top of the landing was a narrow hallway, barely wide enough for two people to walk side by side. The first of the hallway's two doors led to the projection room, and the muffled sounds of John Wayne's distinctive voice wafted through the door. That meant *Rio Bravo* was showing, since the Duke wasn't in *My Darling Clementine*. Not that Nikki gave a damn about Westerns—they were always just about white folks shooting other white folks—but it was impossible to live here without picking up on this stuff.

Nikki reached into her coat's left pocket and pulled out her keys, inserting the proper one into the lock above the knob on the second door on the left.

"Ah, you're back."

"You're up early," Nikki said as she walked through the door. She had hoped Crowley would be asleep on the couch, but he was standing in the kitchenette that took up one wall of the living room, sipping tea from one of Nikki's mugs. The couch hadn't even been opened—when it was, it went from being a living room to a bedroom. The apartment's other room was Robin's.

Bernard Crowley was almost circular. His head was round, with only a thatch of blond hair at the back, the rest having long since fallen out; his cheeks were as chubby as her four-year-old's were when he was born. He had a bit of a potbelly and pasty white skin, all of which made him seem fairly harmless—and this image was not helped by his scratchy voice and British accent. Nikki, though, knew that he was a black belt in karate in addition to being incredibly brilliant.

Of course, he had to be brilliant in order to do his job. He was her Watcher, her mentor, the man who'd found her four years ago and told her that she was the Slayer. *If only he'd found me in time to save Gramma. Or before I met—*

She cut the thought off, as she always did whenever she thought about Robin's father.

The air was stuffy in the room, despite the fan blowing on high in the window that looked out over the bright lights of 42nd Street. The inside of the movie theater itself was air-conditioned, and there were times when Nikki took advantage of its proximity to cool off, but there was only so much Western she could take, so she mostly just lived with the fan.

Crowley ran his hand over his bald head. "Haven't been to sleep yet, I'm afraid. How did it go this evening?"

"Went fine," Nikki said with a grin as she shrugged out of her coat, tossing it onto the battered old easy chair she'd pulled off the street years ago. "Staked two vamps, saved a girl." Nikki sat down on her grandmother's rocking chair and unlaced her platforms. "How's Robin?"

Crowley sat his rotund form on the couch perpendicular to Nikki and pulled a cigarette out of a case in his shirt pocket. "Resting comfortably, thank you, which is nothing short of miraculous given the cinematic balderdash bleeding through the walls. I suspect if the Soviets ever do drop the bomb, Robin will sleep through it."

"Good. Thanks for keeping an eye on him." Nikki wiggled her toes, free of the footwear.

"My pleasure, of course. Still—" Crowley hesitated, lit his cigarette, took a puff on it, then exhaled the smoke. "I would like to, for the seven hundredth time, remind you that I have a very spacious flat on Central Park West—one I never see, by the way, what with taking care of Robin while you're patrolling—and I'd be happy to—"

"No." Nikki leaned forward in the rocking chair, the curved wood creaking on the linoleum floor. "I told you, I ain't livin' in no honkytown. I gotta be the Slayer, that's cool, but I'm gonna be the Slayer for my people."

"All right." Crowley took another sip of tea, which he usually did when he wanted to hide his annoyance. Nikki always thought that was a stupid habit, since all it did was shine a big spotlight on his annoyance. But she didn't care. They'd been having this argument for four years, and they'd probably have it for another four years. The fact was, vamps preyed on the weak and disenfranchised, and in this town, that meant minorities. Besides, Nikki wasn't about to abandon her people. Folks up on the Upper West Side had money and being white on their side; in Hell's Kitchen and Times Square and up in Harlem, they didn't have jack.

In a tight voice, Nikki said, "Look, if you don't want to take care of Robin—"

"Don't be ridiculous." Crowley gave her a look that made Nikki feel like she'd just put a fly in his soup. "I adore your son, you know that. I just think that he—and you—would be safer—"

"Nobody knows who I am, Crowley. Nobody knows where I live. They can't be lookin' me up, 'cause I ain't in the Yellow Pages under 'slayer.' And nobody would think to look in this dump, anyhow— s'why I took it when old man Manguson offered it. Ain't no fit place to live—so it's perfect for the mission. We're all safe here."

"I suppose you're right," Crowley said in that long-suffering tone that meant he *didn't* think she was right but was tired of arguing. He put the mug down on the end table—okay, the wooden crate she used as an end table—and asked, "Anything noteworthy about the two vampires?"

"Lousy fashion sense." Nikki leaned back, setting the chair into a steady rocking motion, grateful that Crowley had changed the subject. She hadn't budged on this position and never would, and she really wished her Watcher would get the hell off it already. "Not a lot to tell—just two cats pickin' on some girl. I stopped 'em."

"Not working with Reet, then?" Crowley asked, blowing out some more smoke.

Nikki shrugged. "Not so's I could tell, but I was

too busy stakin' 'em to ask. They didn't look like Reet's usual muscle, but that don't mean nothin'." Another shrug. "Shoot, if they vamps in this town, they probably got *somethin'* goin' with Reet."

"Sad but true." Crowley got up from the couch, putting out his cigarette in the pottery ashtray Robin had made in nursery school. "Well, I must be going. My own bed, and the blessed silence of a flat not next to a projection room, await my pleasure. Have a good night."

Nikki was too tired to get up from her chair, so she just said, "G'night, Crowley. Sleep good."

She grinned as he winced at her improper grammar. Most of the time he let it slide, but that type of misuse always got his goat. *Well, he deserves it, trying to get me to move on up to his deluxe apartment in the sky. I'm staying here, and he knows it. So why he gotta keep throwing it in my face?*

As he approached the door, he said, "Tomorrow I'd like very much to go over your kicks. I've noticed you're not getting full power behind them." He looked down at her platforms, sitting next to the couch. "Probably has something to do with that ridiculous footwear."

"I *hope* you're not telling me to get new shoes. It's part of the *look*. I gotta look *bad*, Crowley, or else—"

Crowley held up a hand. She'd been making this point to him as much as he'd been harping on moving to his pad. "Yes, of course, striking fear into the hearts of evildoers with your supercool threads. What *was* I thinking? Either way, we need to review kicks—if for no other reason than to take full advantage of those outsize heels of yours."

"Yeah, okay." She was just jiving Crowley, anyhow. She enjoyed the physical training with him. They usually did it in Central Park, where they had some open space, and where Robin could play.

"Good night, Nikki." With that, Crowley left. She could hear his footfalls creaking on the staircase heading down to the theater.

The strains of Ricky Nelson and Dean Martin singing "My Rifle, My Pony and Me" were sounding through the wall when Nikki finally managed to haul herself to her feet and go to the door that led to the apartment's other room.

Robin didn't even budge when the light from the living room shone into his darkened room. Not that a room with a window looking out on Times Square was ever completely dark. Another fan blew in that window as well, in an attempt to keep the stale air moving.

Her little boy's stomach rose and fell slowly, his arms gripping his GI Joe. On the wall was a giant Star Wars poster, which had recently replaced the Evel Knievel poster for the top spot over his bed. Nikki hadn't been able to complain. She'd been the same four years ago when *Cleopatra Jones* came out—especially since she now lived a life eerily similar to Cleo's. The only difference was, everybody knew who Cleo was—she was a badass secret agent. Nikki was a badass, too, with even better moves than Cleo had, but nobody knew who the Slayer really was. From what Crowley told her, that was typical for Slayers, but for Nikki it was a necessity. The mission was all-important, but she wouldn't let it endanger her son. So folks only knew her as the Vampire Slayer, if they knew anything. Her legend had grown over the past four years, which only made it less likely that anyone would find her.

She walked over to the bed and touched Robin's smooth cheek. She loved her little boy more than anything else in the whole world, so she had to keep him safe. Her life wouldn't allow her to do anything else. Crowley had also said that Slayers with children were not the norm, and nothing in his books—his apartment was lined floor to ceiling with them—said anything about what happened to any Slayers who might have got knocked up.

Nikki wasn't letting *anything* happen to her little boy.

But she wasn't gonna give up the mission, either. Robin understood that the mission was what mattered. If Nikki ever doubted it, she just had to remember the looks on the faces of the people she saved.

She was a hero. No way would she give that up.

Giving her son a kiss on the cheek, she went back out into the living room, unfolded the couch, and collapsed on the sofa bed, having earned herself a good night's—or day's—sleep.

As she drifted into dreamland, she thought about the day Crowley had found her four years earlier. . . .

Chapter Three

**New York City
February 10, 1973
10:20 p.m.**

There were few places on Earth dingier than New York City three days after a snowstorm. The day of the storm itself, it was beautiful, like the city was covered in a white blanket. But once the storm stopped and the plows went through, people trod on the snow, and cars and trucks and buses rolled over it belching their fumes, the city became a dreary, ugly place, the snow laced with filth.

Having been born and raised in London, Bernard Crowley knew from dreary, ugly places. The island of Manhattan on this bitter winter evening certainly cracked his top ten.

Bernard ran a hand through his thinning blond hair as he walked down Lenox Avenue, hoping to God the Watchers Council had their facts right. True, they'd been finding and training Slayers for centuries, but when that girl in Poland died, none of the potential Slayers they had in their charge had been activated. Which meant the new Slayer needed to be sought out.

The mystics the Council sometimes employed insisted that the new Slayer was here, in Harlem. Bernard had moved to New York some years ago to observe its rather entrenched vampire population, not to mention the city's various magical hot spots, such as the 125th Street fault line, Ewen Park in the Bronx, and both the North Woods and the Sheep Meadow in Central Park. As a result, he was assigned to find and train this new Slayer.

Is it asking so much for the Slayer to live in a better neighborhood? Bernard's white face stood out like a beacon in Harlem, and while he could take care of himself in a fight, he'd just as soon not put his black belt to good use.

Turning the corner onto 118th Street, he was distressed to see several police cars, lights flashing, and yellow crime-scene tape flapping in the biting winter wind right in front of the very building he was to visit.

He paused and pulled out a cigarette, cupping his hands around the end so the strong winds wouldn't blow out his lighter. *Perhaps it might be best if I return tomorrow.* But Bernard dismissed that thought quickly. It was quite possible that whatever the police were doing here related to the newly activated Slayer. A girl finding herself with super-strength and stamina could very easily get into mischief of some sort. *I'll need to make sure my Slayer isn't in trouble.*

He smiled. *My Slayer. I rather like the sound of that, actually.* Being assigned a Slayer was the highest honor a Watcher could be given, and while Bernard knew it was only because of an accident of geography—no other Watcher was within a hundred miles of New York—he still felt rather chuffed by the whole thing.

Let's just hope that bauble works as well as Kapsis said it would.

As soon as he neared the crime-scene tape, a uniformed constable—or, as they called them here, officer—approached, holding up a gloved hand. "I'm sorry, sir, but you need to step back."

Reaching into his pocket, Bernard pulled out the orb Kapsis had shipped to him. "My name's Crowley—Agent Bernard Crowley, with Interpol. I've received word that this might relate to an investigation of ours. Who's the officer in charge?"

The officer, whose nameplate read O'MALLEY, stared at the orb, blinked for a moment, then stared at Bernard with a look of mild irritation. "This is just an old lady getting iced, Agent Crowley. Ain't no international conspiracies here."

Bernard let out a sigh of relief. The orb did indeed look like an Interpol badge to O'Malley. Taking an imperious puff of his cigarette, he said, "That's for me to judge, I'm afraid. Now then, the officer in charge?" To accentuate his point, he dropped the cigarette onto the sidewalk and stepped on it authoritatively.

With obvious reluctance, O'Malley held up the tape for Bernard to more easily bend under it. He led Bernard up the cracked stoop into the dark, filthy lobby and then up the two flights of stairs to the depressingly small flat, where forensics specialists and officers and plainclothes detectives did their jobs, dusting the various bits of furniture for fingerprints. The couch was at an odd angle to the wall, one of the chairs was upside down, and the shattered remains of a wooden table were strewn all over the floor.

Also on the floor, a man in a blue topcoat and with a cigarette dangling from his mouth was examining an old black woman who was very obviously dead. She had two bloody puncture wounds in her neck.

Bernard knew instantly from looking at her how she'd died. The coroner would no doubt say it was exsanguination from a wound in the carotid artery, but Bernard had a more basic explanation, one the NYPD was unlikely to subscribe to: The old woman had been killed by a vampire.

Off to the side, sitting on an old rocking chair, was a young girl of about fifteen or sixteen years of age. She wore a light blue waitress's uniform commonly seen on employees of diners. Tears streamed down her cheeks, and she was holding a newborn baby in her arms. At first she seemed to be a grieving child, or perhaps grandchild, but Bernard saw something else.

It was her brown eyes. They blazed with a fury that gave Bernard pause.

He suspected that this was his Slayer.

Is the child hers? That's a bit of a nuisance. Still, I'll cross that bridge when I burn it. He forced his attention back to O'Malley, who was introducing him to one of the detectives, a big-nosed, curly-haired, mustachioed man wearing unfashionably small spectacles and a simple suit.

"Detective Landesberg, this is Agent Crawley from Interpol."

"Crowley, actually," Bernard said, offering his hand to the detective. "A pleasure."

"This is a little under your radar, isn't it, Agent Crowley?" Landesberg asked, returning the handshake. Bernard noted that he had a firm grip.

"Perhaps, but I need to verify that for myself. Should I assume that the victim died of exsanguination from wounds in the carotid artery?"

"Coroner's still withholding a final, but that's what it looks like, yeah. Vic's name is Mavis Wood. She lives with her granddaughter, Nikki, and little Robin there." Landesberg pointed at the girl on the easy chair and the baby even as he consulted his notepad. "Nikki's parents were mugged and killed seven years ago. She's been working at a diner to pay the rent—dropped out of school."

That bodes ill, Bernard thought, but he said nothing. "May I speak to the girl?"

"Knock yourself out, but I warn you, she's a little kooky." Landesberg grinned. "She says a vampire killed her grandmother, and that she killed the vampire. Funny that there's no vampire body to go with the story."

Hardly, since vampires don't leave dead bodies behind. Of course, Bernard could not share that knowledge with the detective. "Thank you for the warning. Excuse me."

Bernard moved over to sit down on the armrest of the displaced couch. "Hello—I'm Bernard Crowley. They tell me your name is Nikki Wood. Is that short for Nicole?"

Nikki looked up at Bernard through tear-filled eyes. "Nah, it's just Nikki. Ain't short for nothin'."

He peered down at the bundle in her arms. "Is that your brother?"

"My son, Robin. I named him after my dad."

I was afraid of that. "I see."

"You ain't no fuzz, are you?"

"Very perceptive, Miss Wood—no, I'm not. The, ah, 'fuzz' think I'm from the International Police, but I'm actually with an organization known as the Watchers."

"Yeah? What do you watch?"

"Any number of things—at present, I have my eye on you. I believe, Miss Wood, that you have a destiny."

"Say what?"

"Do you claim that a vampire killed your grandmother?"

Nikki looked away. "You gonna laugh at me too?"

"Actually, no. In fact, I can tell you how it happened. You came home from your job at the diner to find the vampire feeding on your grandmother—or perhaps it had already fed, and your grandmother was dead. In any event, you fought back and were surprised by your own strength. Indeed, it's probably not the first example of increased strength you've observed in yourself of late."

Eyes widening, Nikki nodded slowly and spoke in a low voice. "At the diner, I almost broke my locker. I did dent it a little. Mr. Petalas was mad."

"So you engaged the vampire. At one point you committed some action—a punch or a throw, perhaps—that shattered that end table. Eventually you killed the vampire by stabbing it through the heart with one of the shards from the end table, then called the police."

Now Nikki looked at Bernard again, her brown eyes wide. "How—how'd you know all that? I didn't tell the cops all that stuff."

"Yes, well, I've had some experience with vampires. And very soon, so will you. You see, Nikki, you're the Slayer. That's the destiny I mentioned before. In every generation, a girl is born who fights vampires, demons, and creatures of the night. When one dies, another is chosen. A Slayer died recently, and *you* were chosen. You are now the Slayer, Miss Wood."

Snorting, Nikki said, "Yeah? Any bread in bein' a Slayer? 'Cause if not, you can count me out."

That rather surprised Bernard. Slayers who were called before they'd been recruited as potentials by the Council were often skeptical of their calling, but he wasn't expecting quite this reaction. "I beg your pardon?"

"Only way we survived was me workin' at the diner. Gramma's social security paid the rent; my waitressin' paid for everything else, and Gramma watched Robin. Without Gramma, how'm I gonna survive? Can't feed two mouths *and* pay for this pad. Ain't got no family left now."

Realizing that a call to the Council was going to be in order, Bernard said, "I believe I might be able to help there." He reached into his suit jacket's inner pocket and pulled out a business card. "Once the police are finished with you—however long that might take—I want you to call that number. If you don't reach me directly, an answering service will take your message. Then we can talk further about your destiny."

Still cradling the baby with one arm, she reached out and took the card with the other. "What you're sayin' sounds crazy, you know that."

Bernard smiled. "So does what you're saying. But we both know that it's true." He got up from the armrest. "By the way, how'd you know to stake the vampire in the heart?"

She shrugged. "Wild guess. S'what Peter Cushing always does to Christopher Lee."

Another life saved by Hammer Films. Will wonders never cease. Bernard shook his head with amusement. "Excuse me."

He went over to Landesberg, who was smoking a cigarette and conferring with one of the uniformed officers.

"You get anything useful, Agent Crowley?" Smoke burst out of Landesberg's mouth as he spoke.

"Miss Wood isn't a suspect, is she, Detective?"

Landesberg shook his head. "Nah, neighbors say

some guy broke into the apartment. They heard him struggle with the grandmother, then saw the girl come home, and they heard the fight. Guy got away, obviously, and we don't have a good description on him. Doesn't look good for tracking him down. Unless you know something?"

Bernard did, of course, but he ignored the leading question as he had ignored Landesberg's earlier one and said, "Well, thank you for your cooperation, Detective. Sorry to have bothered you."

"So this wasn't a help," Landesberg said before Bernard could walk off.

"Not the way I'd hoped, no."

"Then why'd you give her a card?"

Giving the detective a little smile, Benard said, "I'm sorry, I can't discuss it," which was true as far as it went.

The next morning Bernard was woken out of a sound sleep by a phone call. This wouldn't have been so bad if he hadn't been up half the night researching the creature that the Council insisted was going to be appearing in the North Woods tomorrow—or, rather, today—at noon. "It's Nikki Wood. You said I'm the Slayer."

"Er, well, yes, that's right." Bernard was having trouble focusing. He hadn't had his tea yet, and it was always touch and go in the old cranium without tea.

"Okay. That mean I get to kill turkeys like the one who killed Gramma?"

"In fact, that will be your *raison d'être*. Your job

will be to slay vampires. Hence, you know—Slayer."

"Right on, Mr. Cooley. You got yourself a Slayer."

"It's Crowley, actually." He managed to stretch the phone cord enough to reach his dressing gown and shrug into it. "Tell you what, Miss Wood, why don't you meet me at the West 100th Street entrance to Central Park, and we can talk further."

"Why there?"

He smiled. "You'll see when you get there."

"All right. They gave me the day off from the diner—I can be there in an hour."

Bernard fumbled for his watch on the end table. It was twenty past ten in the morning. *Perfect.* "I'll meet you there, then."

One hour and a half later, Nikki finally approached the corner of 100th Street and Central Park West, pushing a stroller with a sleeping Robin inside. "Oh dear," Bernard said, stepping on the cigarette he'd only half-smoked. "I rather hadn't intended young Robin to come along." If the creature was to appear as scheduled . . .

"I told you I ain't got no bread, man. How'm I supposed to pay for a babysitter?"

What was it she said last night? "Ain't got no family left now." "Very well," he said after a moment. "You have a great deal to learn, Miss Wood—it won't be easy, it will be incredibly dangerous. But it's also necessary—perhaps now, more than ever. Vampires and demons, you see, prey on the weak, and they thrive on chaos. This city has seen its fair share of chaos of late, and I suspect it will only get worse. Your job is to fight that chaos—quite literally."

"How much this gig pay?"

Bernard had been afraid of that question. "I'm afraid it doesn't as such—however," he added quickly when Nikki turned the stroller around and started to walk down Central Park West, "I have spoken with my superiors." He started walking quickly to keep up with her. "You'll be pleased to know that they have agreed to a stipend that will allow you and your son to live comfortably." At that, she stopped walking; Bernard caught up to her. "I have a flat just down the street from here, and you can stay there."

Nikki turned around. "A stipend? Real bread?"

"That's right."

"Robin'll be taken care of?"

"Absolutely."

She broke into a big grin. "Right on, Mr. Crowley. Tell me what I gotta do."

"The first thing you must do is come with me."

Bernard led Nikki into the park, then hung an immediate left, taking them around the duck pond and into the North Woods.

Robin woke up and looked at the pond.

"Those are ducks, Robin," Nikki said with a smile.

"Ba!"

Very soon they were off the paved path and in amongst the trees.

Nikki was having trouble navigating the stroller over the snow-covered dirt. "We supposed to be here?"

Allowing himself a small smile, Bernard looked at his watch. *Just about noon.* "Oh, it's a public park. We can be anywhere we want. Ah, I suggest you continue forward." He turned and walked back behind the stroller. "I'll keep an eye on young Robin here. You go on ahead."

Nikki hesitated. "Only reason I'm trustin' you is 'cause you knew about vampires. If you're messin' with me—"

"I'm not. This is serious business, Miss Wood—we both have a sacred responsibility. Now, you're older than most Slayers are when they're called—and generally, they've had plenty of training." *And no children.* "We'll have to catch you up in fairly short order. It will involve intense training and a great deal of study."

With a snort, Nikki said, "Figured those days was over when I dropped out. Guess not. But still—I'm a lot stronger than I used to be, and it ain't from throwin' plates round the diner. Somethin's happened to me, and you're the cat who knows the score. So I'll buy your rap, Mr. Crowley, but only 'cause I ain't got no choice." She took a breath. "So what do I do?"

"Just keep walking forward."

Nikki did as Bernard asked.

His watch struck noon. Nothing happened. *This will look incredibly foolish if the Council's information was faulty.*

But no, the only thing faulty was his cheap watch—it was fast. Within seconds the air stirred, and a hot wind seemed to come out of nowhere, blowing the dead leaves into a whirlwind on the ground.

Robin started crying. Bernard started sweating—

he was wearing a thick winter coat, but this wind felt like it came straight from the Gobi.

A fissure opened in the very air in front of where Nikki was standing—a portal, and through it came a small creature with green fur, huge fangs, sharp claws, and blood-red eyes. This was the Morvag demon the Council had warned him about.

Seeing Nikki, the beast leaped at her, claws out. Nikki threw up her arms in a defensive posture, which resulted in the Morvag slicing through the sleeves of her down coat. Feathers went flying out into the cold air.

"That was my only coat, you jive turkey!" Nikki lashed out at the Morvag, making up in strength what she lacked in finesse. She punched the creature, knocking it to the leaf-and-snow-and-dirt-covered ground. Then she stepped on its stomach, which caused it to let out an earsplitting howl.

Robin's cries grew worse. Perhaps the child sensed the danger, or perhaps he was just cranky, the way newborn babies were. Either way, the combination of the Morvag's howling and the boy's crying was giving Bernard a headache right behind his left eye.

The Morvag slashed again at Nikki from its prone position, which was enough to get her to dance out of the way and then trip on a tree branch that was lurking under some snow. Nikki fell to the ground as the Morvag got up.

As the Morvag charged at her, Nikki kicked upward at the creature's head, snapping its neck instantly. It fell to the ground, dead.

"That's it?" Nikki sounded almost disappointed.

Bernard raised an eyebrow. "It's—" He winced; Robin was still crying. He raised his voice. "It's your first demon, Miss Wood. Trust me, they get a good deal more difficult. I merely wished to show you what *you* can do."

As she got to her feet and moved back toward the stroller, Nikki said, "What, beat up a green dog?"

"That was no dog, Miss Wood, that was a Morvag demon. While they're minor members of the daemonic pantheon, they are still quite dangerous. And it's not everyone who can break such a creature's neck with one kick."

At that, Nikki grinned. "Yeah, I did do that, didn't I?" She then knelt down at the stroller. "Hey, it's okay, Robin, baby, Mama's here." She started to reach for her son, then noticed the shreds that were all that remained of her coat's sleeves. Shrugging out of the coat and letting it fall to the ground, she then picked up Robin and cradled him in her arms. She seemed completely unaffected by the low temperature, which Bernard thought might well be a by-product of her calling.

After Nikki had cooed at Robin for a few moments, he quieted down. Only then did she look over at Bernard. "So it gets harder, huh?"

"Considerably. As I said, Morvag demons are at the bottom of the food chain, as it were. Most of what you'll be facing will be vampires, like the monster that killed your grandmother."

"Sounds groovy to me, Mr. Crowley." She put Robin back into the stroller. As she buckled it, she said, "I'm gonna need me a new coat."

Chapter Four

**New York City
July 5, 1977
11:15 p.m.**

The air in CBGB's was filled with smoke and sweat and alcohol, and Penny could feel the thrum of the bass guitar in her rib cage. Jacko, the lead singer, screamed into the microphone, the mic's head halfway into his mouth. Next to him, Davey, the lead guitarist, pounded away on the strings—one of which broke at some point during the song, but he kept playing. Donnie was hitting the drums so hard Penny thought his arms would fall off. He was using two bass drums, too, the beat slamming into Penny's toes.

But Penny's eyes were on the source of the vibrations in her ribs: Ricky, the bass player. He had curly blond hair that he cut real close—not all wild like most boys did. That was why Penny loved seeing punk bands like Apple Corpse. They didn't do what other bands did.

She turned to look at her roommate, Phyllis, who was pressed up against the bar next to her. They weren't as close to the stage as Penny would have liked, and they could only see bits and pieces of most of the band members through the crowd in front of them.

But from this angle, they could see Ricky perfectly, which was all Penny cared about.

Penny leaned in to Phyllis's ear and shouted, "Aren't they great?"

Phyllis just shrugged.

Rolling her eyes and sipping her rum and Coke, Penny stared back at Ricky. His zebra-patterned T-shirt was nice and tight, and he looked *so* hip in his leather pants. Somebody squeezed in toward the bar next to her and tried to get the bartender's attention, but she didn't pay him any mind.

When the song came to an end, everyone screamed and applauded, Penny as loudly as anyone.

Jacko screamed into his mic, his distorted voice barely understandable over the PA system. "Thank you, CBGB's!" The cheers got louder. "That was 'Kiss My Teeth.' I wrote that one on the toilet."

"Yeah, we can bloody tell," said someone with a British accent to Penny's left. It was the guy who had squeezed past her. Her knees getting weak at just the sound of that accent, she turned to take a good look at him—

—and instantly fell in love. Not only did he have the accent, but he had blond hair that was even hipper than Ricky's, and he was wearing all black—ripped T-shirt, jeans, and leather with studs.

All thoughts of Ricky fleeing from her brain, Penny asked, "You don't like it?"

"It's bollocks. Give me Sid Vicious any day."

Jacko screamed. "We got one more song to do! It's called 'Bollocks.'"

The blond man winced as he lit a cigarette, striking a match on the bar, which Penny thought was just *so* cool. "Americans should never use the word 'bollocks.' Ever. Should be a bloody rule, it should."

"You have a *really* hip accent."

Penny looked to her right to see that Phyllis was staring at the blond man also. In fact, Penny thought she saw drool coming out of her roommate's mouth.

Whatever other conversation might have followed was drowned out by Donnie slamming on the drums to open up "Bollocks."

Phyllis squeezed past some dude and moved so she was standing between Penny and the stage, which also put her closer to the British guy. She shouted, "What brings you here?"

The blond guy—whose cheekbones were just out of *sight*—leaned in close, giving Penny a great look at his eyes. He had a scar on his left eyebrow, and Penny wondered how he got it. *Probably in a bar fight,* she thought, shivers going up and down her body.

He said, "Heard this was the joint where the Ramones and the Dead Boys and the like got their start. Wanted to see what all the fuss was about."

At that point the bartender came over, and the British guy was ordering a drink. Penny tried to give Phyllis her sternest I-saw-him-first look, but Phyllis only had eyes for the Brit.

"Bollocks" ended, and the place erupted. Jacko screamed, "Thank you, New York!"

Hilly Kristal, the owner of the club, jumped onto the stage. A purple bandanna, sunglasses, and a thick red beard combined to almost completely obscure his face. He wore a black jacket with gold butterflies sewn on the lapels, unzipped to reveal a black T-shirt that said "The Guiding Light," and bright red pants. "All right, you rock and roll animals!" he screamed into the mic. "Open your hind legs and clap your paws for Apple Corpse! Keep your tails in their cages, 'cause next up are the incredible Cryers!"

"That's a sad name," the blond guy said after taking a drag on his cigarette. Then the bartender handed him a pint of beer. "Apple Corpse, I mean. The Cryers ain't bad. Honest, and all that."

"But . . ." Penny hesitated. She wanted to defend Ricky, though she also found that she wasn't caring as much about Ricky right now.

Phyllis jumped in. "It's a play on words. Apple Corpse instead of apple core."

"Yeah, I *get* that—it's pants. Tryin' to sound macabre, but they just end up lookin' like poofters."

Frowning, Penny asked, "What's a poofter? I mean, I can tell it's bad from the way you said it, but—"

"I believe you Yanks use the word 'faggot'—but

that's what I call this thing." He held up his cigarette. "I gotta say, since I met you two, my night has looked up."

Penny felt her heart melt. "Really?"

"You have *really* got it goin' on," Phyllis added.

"I'm called Spike."

"Spike," Penny whispered. It was a great name, one that sounded like violence and passion and all those things that Ricky didn't have. *God, what was I thinking, falling for a bass player? This Spike dude is much hipper.* "I'm Penny." Phyllis elbowed her in the ribs, and she added, "And, uh, this is my roommate, Phyllis."

"Penny and Phyllis?"

The roommates exchanged glances and shy smiles. They always got this. In perfect unison, they said, "Two *P*s in a pod!"

"Bloody charming." Spike took a sip of his beer. "Guh. I keep forgettin' the rules of world travel—never eat the meat in China, never drink the water in Mexico, and never drink the beer in the States." He put the pint down and moved it away. "I thought I'd get to see the bloody Ramones, at least. S'why I came to this dump."

Penny's face brightened. "Oh, they'll be playing on Friday. They're headlining a whole punk weekend."

Phyllis added, "We're planning on coming—maybe we'll see you then."

Spike just took a drag on his cigarette. "Excellent. See, the Ramones, they're a *band*, not like these tossers. Just a buncha words thrown together pretending to be meaningful. It's not poetry, not like what the

Sex Pistols or the Ramones do—or even the Dead Boys."

Her eyes going wide, Phyllis said, "You've *seen* the Sex Pistols?"

Grinning, Spike said, "I have. Plenty o' times."

"Wow. I wish I could see them."

"Well, maybe someday you will, pet."

Why can't he call me *"pet"?* Penny tried not to sulk.

Spike continued, "I don't know about you two, but I could use some air."

Before Penny could answer, she felt a finger tap on her shoulder. She turned to see Ricky standing there. "Hey there, foxy lady. Why didn't you come up to the stage?"

"Oh, uh, well, uh—" Penny didn't know what to say. She was supposed to go back to Brooklyn with Ricky and the rest of the band to that Irish pub they all liked, and then maybe back to his place, but ever since seeing Spike, she realized how shallow and meaningless her crush on Ricky was. He was some really, really good eye candy, but he didn't have any substance to him. Spike, she could tell, was a *real* man.

As if to prove Penny's thoughts correct, Spike stepped forward, putting himself between Penny and Ricky. "The birds're with me, mate."

"'Birds'? What're you, some kinda British fag?"

"No. This," Spike flicked the cigarette into Ricky's face, "is a British fag. And I suggest you back off—now."

Ricky hesitated.

Then Spike leaned in. "I said *now*."

"Yeah, okay," Ricky muttered, and then went back toward the stage.

Penny stared at Spike with loving eyes. Next to her, Phyllis did the same. "Wow, that was *so* out there," she murmured.

"Weren't we gonna get some air?" Spike asked.

"You wanna come back to our pad?" Phyllis asked. "It's not that far—just a quick cab ride."

Spike nodded. "I'm feelin' a bit peckish, actually."

Quickly, Penny said, "There's an all-night Chinese place around the corner." She had been hoping to get Spike to a bar or something first, so she could find a way to ditch Phyllis. Maybe she could pull it off at Chung Wah's.

"And they deliver, too," Phyllis said. "We can order in."

"Sounds good to me, pet," Spike said, putting one arm around Phyllis, and another around Penny. It didn't last, as the club was too crowded for them to make it through three abreast, but they stayed close as they moved to the exit.

Dammit, dammit, dammit. Penny could not catch a break tonight. She'd finally met the man of her dreams, and Phyllis had to horn in on it. *And she's the one who gets called "pet." Twice!*

Jacko was waiting for them when they stepped out onto the sidewalk. The white awning with the CBGB/OMFUG logo and the club's street address hung over them. "Where you takin' them?"

"Not that it's any o' your business, mate, but

they've invited me to their flat for a nightcap. Unless you're givin' me a better offer?" Spike stood nose-to-nose with Jacko.

After a second, Jacko looked away.

God, I can't believe that. He just backed off. If anything, it made Penny feel better about dumping Ricky.

Spike walked past Jacko, being sure to knock into his side as he passed, and raised his arm. A Checker Cab was coming up the Bowery and veered toward the curb to get them. Like a true gentleman, Spike held the door for Penny and Phyllis. Penny got in first and told the cabbie their address.

Then Spike turned to look at Jacko. "By the way, mate—your songs're poxy. You ain't fit to spit on Joey Ramone's shoes."

It wasn't until Spike got in and closed the door that Jacko responded. "Joey Ramone ain't *nothin'*, you hear me? *Nothin'!* Ramones're a flash in the pan, man! You'll see!"

Penny smiled across the rear of the cab at Spike, who was sitting in the rumble seat. "That was *wonderful.*"

"You really showed him," Phyllis added. "Uh, you do like Chinese food, right?"

"Chinese ain't bad—best meal of my life was in China, matter of fact." Spike lit a fresh cigarette. "But I was hoping for something more local tonight."

The flat—or "pad," as the birds called it—was one of the ugliest places Spike had ever laid eyes on in over a century of life. He wasn't sure what disgusted him more: the awful wood paneling, the orange shag carpeting, or the ugly painting over the couch. Then there was the couch itself, which was some color not found in nature.

Spike was partial to all black these days. Colors made him ill.

Still and all, the evening wasn't a total loss. He didn't see the Ramones, but at least they'd be around come Friday. Spike figured his business in the Big Apple would take at least that long.

And I got a nice meal out of it. Two birds in their prime—home delivery, no less. He looked down at the orange-carpeted floor, which now had some red mixed in with it, seeping out from the two corpses piled unceremoniously in the center of the living room—not a lot, of course, as Spike had taken most of the blood from the "two *P*s in a pod" for himself.

I almost bit them right then and there in CB's after they talked in unison like that. But it was so much more fun to take the girls away from their men, especially given that the men in question were such ponces. *Apple bloody Corpse indeed. Oughtta track them down and kill 'em just on general principles. Not even drain their blood— wouldn't want any chance of their stupidity infecting me. Just snap their necks. Or maybe rip their guts out.*

It had been fun to watch the look on Penny's face when Spike vamped out and drained Phyllis. Or was it Penny he drained first? He couldn't remember which *P* was which—and, upon reflection, didn't really give a toss.

He lit a cigarette, dropping the match onto the fake-wood coffee table. Now that he was satiated, and had had some fun in the process, it was time to get to work.

I've got me a Slayer to kill.

Chapter Five

**New York City
July 7, 1977
9:15 p.m.**

Moses "Reet" Weldon looked at Izzy and shook his head. "You disappoint me, Izzy."

Reet was seated behind the oak desk that he'd had for as long as he'd been running the Harlem rackets. Izzy was standing on the other side, shaking. One of Reet's lieutenants, Curtis, stood behind Izzy.

"Look, Mr. Weldon, I ain't jivin' you, it's been rough, and I had to—"

Slamming a hand down on the oak, Reet said, "You *had* to skim? Is that what you're saying to me, boy?"

Izzy stood up straight. "Aw, look, don't be callin' me 'boy,' Mr. Weldon, that ain't right."

"'Boy' is what men call their younger inferiors, and you, Izzy, are both. You're younger by about a hundred years, and inferior by virtue of being human." Reet stood up, straightening the jacket of his charcoal pinstriped suit. "We're barely clearing a profit on weed right now, Izzy. That means every dollar counts. So when I find out that one of my men is taking more than his fair share, I get displeased."

"Look, it's just a loan, Mr. Weldon, honest! I ain't jivin' you, brother, I just—things been a little rough, you know? Times is *hard*, man. But I promise, I'll pay you back—with interest! Just gimme some more *time*, man, okay?"

Reet shook his head. "I'm sorry, Izzy—but I'm not your brother, and time is one thing you don't have. This is the fourth time you've been caught skimming. Now I like to give people second chances, but we've gone beyond that. So I'm afraid I'm going to have to make an example of you."

Izzy's shaking got worse. "Naw, man, look, I'll be good, okay? I'll pay it back—right now, I promise, Mr. Weldon, just lemme—lemme get to my pad and I can—"

"I'm sorry, but it's too late, Izzy. Curtis?"

Curtis smiled.

Looking over at Curtis, Izzy said, "Aw, no, please, don't—"

"Quiet," Curtis said.

Then his face changed.

Curtis grabbed Izzy by his Afro and yanked his head back, exposing his neck. Then he bit down and fed off Izzy while his worthless body convulsed.

Before Izzy completely shuffled off this mortal coil, Curtis looked up, blood on his mouth. "I'm sorry, Reet, did you want some?"

Shaking his head, Reet said, "No thank you, Curtis, I already ate. Besides, I doubt he would agree with me."

Laughing, Curtis finished feeding, then let Izzy's corpse drop to the linoleum floor. When Reet had bought this Lenox Avenue building fifteen years ago, the room had shag carpet, but it was damn near impossible to get bloodstains out, so he'd pulled it up and replaced the floor. His cleaning staff had been grateful.

Reet was less concerned with the monetary angle of Izzy's skimming. The decline of the hippie subculture had meant a steady reduction in demand for marijuana. Heroin and cocaine were the drugs of choice these days, and that was where Reet made his money, along with the numbers and gambling and prostitution. No, taking care of Izzy was more a case of cutting off a dead branch to keep the tree from getting sick.

"I'll get the boys to take care o' this cat," Curtis said, his face reverting.

"Good. Is there anything else? Martha's singing at the club tonight."

"We got three new places under our protection—deli on Tenth and Forty-fifth, fruit and vegetable stand on Fifty-seventh and Ninth, and an auto parts joint on Amsterdam and Seventy-third. Figure we oughtta be scorin' three bills more a week at least."

"Good," Reet said. While "protection" scams had a

certain simple vulgarity to them, they were often very profitable. Besides, there were times when Reet liked simple vulgarity. "I take it those places were cleared by the Gambinos?"

Curtis nodded. "Yeah, the guineas're cool with it."

"Good," Reet said again. For his operations in Harlem, Reet was left alone, but any expansions south of 110th Street had to be cleared with the Italians. Reet had learned the hard way to respect the Cosa Nostra. "Anything else?"

"Marv and Gene brought Mikey in—along with Mikey's new pal."

Reet sighed. He'd forgotten about that. "All right, once you've removed Izzy, send them in."

Curtis nodded, picked up the phone on Reet's desk, and dialed four numbers that connected him to another line in the building. "It's Curtis. Get Hobie and Georgie up here."

Once those two—who had been quite strong even before they were turned into vampires, which was why Curtis often gave them the heavy lifting—took Izzy's corpse away, Reet pushed the button on his intercom and told Marv and Gene to bring Mikey in, but not the other one.

Mikey Gitlin was white, and pasty-looking even by vampire standards. He'd been working for Reet for the last ten years or so. Marv and Gene, two of his human employees, each held a cross and stood on either side of Mikey to make sure he didn't go anywhere.

"Mikey," Reet said, "how many times have I told you, you don't turn somebody without checking first?"

"I'm—I'm sorry, Mr. Weldon, I dunno what come over me. I wasn't—I wasn't thinking, man, I just—I just—"

Reet held up a hand. "Mikey, we have rules here, rules that I know you're familiar with." He opened the humidor on his desk and took out one of his Cubans. "You see, I provide services to our community." Of course, some would view the drugs, gambling, sex, and enforcement he provided to be something other than "services," but those were merely the opinions of humans. Reet hadn't cared about what humans thought since the end of the Civil War. "I do this with a network of vampires. But we creatures of the night are— unpredictable." He ran the cigar under his nose, closing his eyes and pausing a moment to enjoy the olfactory delight of a well-made Cuban. Of course, it had been illegal to import cigars into the United States since Castro took over Cuba eighteen years ago, but Reet had plenty of extralegal sources at his disposal.

After clipping off one end of the cigar, Reet walked around the desk, keeping his deep voice at an even tone. "The way I'm able to manage things is to keep a strict limit on the vampire population of the city. We are demons, after all, cohabitating with the remnants of the personalities we had in life. It's hard enough to maintain a racket without having unexpected demons gumming up the works. Do you understand what I'm saying, Mikey?"

Mikey was shaking even more than Izzy had been. "I—I know, Mr. Weldon, I'm sorry, I just—"

Reet raised an eyebrow. "Just what?"

Mikey kept shaking, but didn't say anything. Reet looked over at Marv and nodded.

Stepping forward, Marv grabbed Mikey's right wrist and applied the cross to his right hand. Mikey screamed, stumbling to his knees as his hand caught fire, but Marv maintained his grip, so Mikey's hand was still at about Reet's chest level, even with the hand's owner on his knees.

Leaning down, Reet placed the cigar into his mouth, sticking the other end into the flames that danced up from Mikey's right hand. He puffed a few times, savoring the taste of the cigar. Then he stood upright, inhaled the sweetness of the Cuban for a moment while enjoying the sounds of Mikey's agonized wails, and nodded to Marv, who released Mikey's wrist and stepped back.

Frantically, Mikey patted down his right hand with his left, putting out the small fire on his flesh.

Looking down at Mikey's whimpering form, Reet repeated himself. "Just *what*?"

"It—it's my brother, Mr. Weldon, okay? He's sick, and the doctors don't know what's wrong with him an' he's gonna die an' I had to do *something*, so I made him a vampire so he won't be sick no more!"

Reet blinked. "It's your brother?"

Mikey was clutching his hand and wincing with every word he spoke. "Yessir, I swear it is, Mr. Weldon, he was sick before an' now he's all better!"

Looking over at Gene, Reet said, "Bring him in."

Gene nodded and went out to the waiting room outside Reet's office.

"I promise, Mr. Weldon, you won't be sorry. He's a good man, my brother, really—he'll make a good soldier. He fought in the war, you know."

"He was in Nam?" Reet asked.

"Uh, no—Second World War. Fought in the Pacific."

Gene led a stooped old man into the office. He had to be at least ninety years old.

No wonder the doctors didn't know what was wrong with him—too many things to choose from. Reet had seen what old age did to his mother back on the plantation in Mississippi, and every night before he went to bed he thanked his sire for sparing him that fate. He knew he'd die eventually—he'd seen too many fellow bloodsuckers get dusted, and lately there was the Slayer cutting a swath through his people—but it would be on his feet, like a man.

He looked down at Mikey, who was still on his knees, clutching his burned hand. "You turned *this*?"

"He's my *brother*, Mr. Weldon. My baby brother, and I always promised our mama I'd take care of him."

Unbidden, a century-old image slammed into Reet's consciousness: a middle-aged black man hanging from a tree on the Weldon plantation, fresh whip scars all across his back.

The corpse had been named Abraham, and in life he had been a slave, property of the Weldons, just like his brother, Moses. But Moses had run away, promising that he'd come back for Abe some day. When that day—or night, rather, for Moses had been turned by that point—had finally arrived, it had been too late.

The Weldons had meted out their idea of justice on Moses's brother.

The old man shook Gene off and stared down at Mikey. "And *this* is how you take care of me? You turn me into a vampire, you little punk? Bad enough I gotta watch you suck people dry, now you turn me into one of your filthy kind?" He spit on his brother.

"Joey, how can you say that?" Mikey was crying now. "I wanted to save you—"

"You call *this* saving?"

"But—"

Reet took a puff on his cigar, then set it down on the glass ashtray on his desk. "That's enough!"

Both men quieted down.

"You thought this would work on me, didn't you, Mikey? You knew the rules—that no one gets turned without permission—but you figured the boss had a soft spot for people who wanted to save their brothers, and you thought it would be easier to obtain my forgiveness after the fact than my permission before it."

"I—I figured you'd understand, Mr. Weldon. My brother, he—"

Having heard more than enough, Reet nodded to Gene, who pulled a stake out of his leather jacket pocket.

Joey was dust a second later.

Mikey's eyes went wide. "No! You killed my brother!"

"We have enough vampires who don't want to be undead. I've no use for any more."

Collapsing to the linoleum floor, Mikey whimpered, "Can't believe you killed him."

"Believe it." Reet nodded to Marv, who removed a stake of his own.

The floor was covered in dust a second later.

Reet shook his head. "Such a waste. Anything else I need to know about?"

Marv nodded. "Yeah, boss, Leroy's outside. Says he's got somethin' to say."

Sighing, Reet sat back down at his desk. If it were anyone else, he would let it wait until later, but Leroy was his right hand. He didn't have anything to say to Reet that wasn't important. "All right, get him in here. I'm missing my music every second we waste with this."

Leroy came in a moment later, dressed in a purple jacket covering a white shirt with ruffled cuffs that stuck out past the jacket's sleeves and skintight pants that matched the jacket. Reet couldn't help but wince at the getup. But then, he'd never had much use for any fashions. He only wore the suit because it conveyed authority, but he'd just as soon wear the rags he wore as a slave as long as he stayed undead and well.

As usual, Leroy didn't waste time with preliminaries. "Our dudes on the fuzz got news. There's two girls got themselves killed downtown a couple days back."

"Girls get killed downtown all the time, especially since that fool with the forty-four started his spree. I'm missing Martha—" Reet started to get up.

Then Leroy said, "They was iced by a bloodsucker."

Reet sat back down. "One of ours?"

Shaking his head, Leroy said, "Nah, boss. Description the fuzz got is of a honky Brit. Blond hair, all spiky like them punk dudes."

Picking up the cigar from the ashtray, Reet took a long drag on it. "Send Heathcliff and Shades—I want to know who this man is. If he's just passing, we'll let him be. If he plans to remain a while, then he is to be recruited. I won't have stragglers in my town. And if he resists recruitment, then he's dust." He smiled. "You dig?"

"I most surely do, boss. I'm on it like stink on cheese."

"Good." Reet took a final puff, then put the cigar out in the ashtray. "Now then, I have a show to attend."

Moses Weldon had been born in 1830. His deeply religious parents had given both their children names from the Bible, and they had always believed that Jesus would save them. Moses hadn't been willing to wait for Jesus to get around to it, however. In 1865, when the tide of the War Between the States had turned to favor the Union, he had run away. His father had been sold to another plantation and died of old age while there. His mother died shortly after getting word that her husband had died so far away from her. Moses had hoped to bring Abe with him, but Abe insisted on staying behind and covering his younger brother's tracks.

While on the road, Moses had come across another runaway named Caleb, and they had run together through the night. At daybreak they had both gone into hiding, but Caleb had refused to come out at all, not even to steal food. That night Caleb's face had changed, and he had pounced on Moses's neck, his suddenly huge canine teeth biting down. When he finished, he opened one of his own veins and fed Moses with his own blood.

The next day Moses had experienced a freedom greater than anything he'd ever known or imagined.

Caleb kept running north, but Moses had power now. The Weldons could no longer threaten him. They had separated his parents, they had treated their human property worse than their furniture, and they had driven Moses to run away.

Now he could get his revenge. And also rescue Abe.

But when he returned to the plantation late one night, he found Abe's corpse hung from a tree. The Weldons had punished Abe for Moses's sin of trying to be free.

So Moses had punished them.

Reveling in his vampiric power, and furious with his inability to save his brother, Moses had taken his sweet time with the Weldons. Their suffering had been ten times worse than the beatings they had inflicted on their slaves over the years.

He had given them each the day to recover, while he hid from the burning sunlight. Then he tortured them anew through the night.

After three days, they had finally died. Christopher, the owner who had sold Moses's father rather than see two slaves be happy. Annabelle, Christopher's wife, who had ordered more beatings than all the other white people on the plantation combined, sometimes for so simple an offense as spilling a drop of her tea. William, their oldest son, who had regularly changed the quotas to guarantee that the slaves would never meet them. And their youngest son, John, who had served as overseer and had taken pleasure in every whipping he had been ordered to bestow.

With the death of his owners and the Union's victory in the war, Moses had become a free man in every respect. He wandered for many years, eventually winding up in New York City around the turn of the twentieth century. It was there that he had obtained the nickname "Reet" due to his fondness for the music of Cab Calloway, in particular the song "Are You All Reet?" He had seen Calloway at New York's Cotton Club, and Moses loved the music. That record had been the first one he had ever bought after obtaining a record player, and he played it so much he wore out two needles and three copies of the LP.

Eventually, Reet worked his way up to the top of the Harlem rackets, using brains and skill—and, whenever that failed, his vampiric ability to kill, maim, torture, and not die when shot or stabbed—to make it to the top of the heap.

He also slowly took control of a large chunk of the vampire population in Manhattan. Most bloodsuckers were followers; sheep, really, who were more than happy to take the direction of whatever shepherd came their way. Reet Weldon had provided that direction, and he kept things under control—or, at least, he had until the Slayer had come to town.

Reet had heard his first stories about the Slayer

from Caleb, but he hadn't put much stock in them until one had actually shown up in the city in 1912, a decade after Reet arrived. But there hadn't been a Slayer in town since the early 1950s.

The current one, though, whatever her name was—and Reet would pay good money to learn that piece of information—had been, as the saying went, bad news. In four years, she'd done everything she could to tear down Reet's organization. Reet was unconcerned, however. He'd survived far worse than one girl in his time. He'd survive this Slayer, too.

Reet had taken many lessons from his time as a piece of property. One was how *not* to run a business. The Weldons had treated their slaves poorly, which had resulted in poor farming, which had resulted in less money for the plantation owners. That turned into a vicious circle, because that had just led to harsher treatment, which had in turn led to worse farming and even less money. Reet ran his business better than that, which was why, ultimately, the Slayer wasn't a huge worry.

Still, there were times when the equivalent of a whipping was necessary. Hence the deaths of Izzy, Mikey, and Mikey's elderly brother.

And, if necessary, this new British vampire.

Chapter Six

**New York City
July 8, 1977
4:05 p.m.**

On Friday morning Nikki woke up to the sound of dramatic music—not the muffled noise that usually came from the Gem, but the nearer sounds of the little black-and-white TV they kept in Robin's bedroom. Frowning, she looked over at the alarm clock and was not entirely surprised to see that it, in fact, wasn't Friday morning, it was late Friday afternoon. The previous night had been a long one, as a Fyarl demon had gotten loose on the Columbia University campus—apparently it was in the service of one of the psychology professors. Took Nikki forever to find something made out of silver to kill the thing with, and then she had to torch the prof's bookcase to take care of his spell books. She didn't get back to the Gem until well after dawn.

Bless his heart, Robin kept himself busy with his comic books, TV, and some cereal. Here in the heart of Times Square, the TV antenna could only get two stations clearly—channels 11 and 13. Mostly Robin watched the latter, which was the local PBS station, but late afternoons Channel 11, an independent station, showed reruns of *Batman*, *Superman*, and *The Lone Ranger*. Robin loved superhero stories because, as he put it, "They remind me of you, Mama!"

Still wearing the blouse and jeans she'd had on the night before, but in bare feet, Nikki padded into the bedroom to see Robin sitting on the floor, his back against the bed, staring up at George Reeves jumping out a window. A *Defenders* comic book was open on his lap. "What's happenin', baby boy?"

Robin looked up and leaped to his feet, the comic book falling to the floor. "You're up!" He ran over and hugged Nikki's legs.

"Yeah, I'm up. What you doin'?"

"Nothin'. Jus' readin' my new comic books and watchin' TV. Mister Rogers went to the Land of Make-Believe again."

Nikki smiled, glad that Robin enjoyed *Mister Rogers' Neighborhood*—not to mention *Sesame Street* and *The Electric Company*—as much as he enjoyed the superheroes. She wanted her boy to have an imagination, and smarts. That was why she was so glad Crowley encouraged him. *I may be the Slayer, but my boy's gonna be more than that. He'll be a writer or a teacher or something.*

She and Robin sat and talked for a little while in the bedroom. Then they went out to the living room, where he helped her fold the bed back up into a couch. After that, he stood next to her in the kitchenette while she scrambled herself a couple of eggs—the last two eggs, as it happened; they'd need to go shopping some time soon—and brewed some coffee, fighting with the Mr. Coffee which never worked right. Throughout, Robin told her all about what was happening with the Avengers and Spider-Man and the Defenders in his comic books, and how Batman got out of the Riddler's trap on TV. "But it wasn't the real Riddler, Mama. It was some other guy that dressed like him—he looked like Gomez Addams."

Laughing, Nikki said, "They just got a different actor, baby boy. It's the same guy who played Gomez."

"I like the other guy better."

"Me too. So how'd Batman get out of it?"

Robin explained how the cliffhanger got resolved while Nikki ate her eggs and drank her coffee. By the time they were done, it was almost five thirty.

"Robin, I gotta go out for a while."

Sounding disappointed, Robin said, "But Mama—"

Giving her son a stern look, Nikki said, "Now what did I tell you, Robin?" She put a hand on his shoulder. "Mama has a mission. And the mission is what matters."

Robin nodded quickly. "I know. I just—I was likin' talkin' to you, is all."

"I know, baby boy, I know." She ran her hand through his hair. "We'll talk more tomorrow, okay?"

"Can we go to the zoo?"

Nikki considered. "Maybe—if it doesn't rain."

"It's not gonna rain." Robin sounded as sure as only a four-year-old could. "Can we go to the Bronx Zoo? I wanna go to Wild Asia."

"We'll see, baby boy," Nikki said. Ever since Robin had heard about the new Wild Asia monorail ride in the Bronx Zoo, he'd been eager to go. "I'm gonna go out and see what's on the grapevine for the weekend. If we can go up to the Bronx, we will—otherwise, we'll go to Central Park."

His face lighting up, Robin asked, "If we go to Central Park, can we ride the carousel?"

"You bet."

"Outta sight and dy-no-mite!"

Smiling at her son's optimism, Nikki got up, put the dishes in the tiny sink, and then grabbed the phone off the wall. Dialing Crowley's number, she said to Robin, "I just gotta check in."

After one ring, Crowley's distinctive voice said, "Hallo?"

"What's happenin', Crowley, it's me."

"Well, that's rather fortuitous. I was about to call you to see if you'd managed to rouse yourself."

"Hey, Fyarl demons are tough work."

"Indeed. Though I was under the impression that it was silver that killed them, not fire."

Nikki let out a breath through her teeth. "Be cool, Crowley, I didn't have no choice—that professor cat was one jive mother—" She cut herself off, not wanting to curse in front of Robin. "He said he wasn't sorry, and he was just gonna summon another one."

"He really said that?" Crowley managed to sound outraged, angry, and surprised at the same time. Nikki figured that was something they taught at Watcher School.

"Yeah. Oh, but he said this time he'd summon one that's more docile."

"There's no such thing as a docile Fyarl demon."

"Yeah, that's what I said." Nikki reached up into the cupboard above the sink and pulled out a glass. It was filthy, so she placed it in the sink and grabbed another one that was mostly clean, then filled it with cold water from the tap. "The cat didn't listen, so I grabbed the Zippo he was lightin' them stinky cigarettes with and lit up his bookcase."

"That was very rash, Nikki. Do you know what might've happened?"

"I ain't stupid, Crowley, I made sure the fire didn't spread." She took a sip of her water.

"It's not that—certain grimoires react very badly to being lit on fire. You could've caused a horrible explosion or opened a dimensional portal or something. In any event," he said quickly before Nikki could protest, "what's done is done. Let's move on. I've got news."

Wincing, Nikki said, "Don't tell me it's St. Vigeous again. Last time, I was sore for two weeks from all the bloodsuckers."

"That won't be for a few months yet. I'm afraid I

don't have the specifics. I've just received a call from Detective Landesberg. I'm going to meet him at that diner he likes, and I'll get the skinny, as it were, there."

"Great," Nikki muttered, gulping down some more water.

Crowley sighed. "Look, Nikki, I know you don't like the police, but Arthur—"

"You're callin' that honky 'Arthur' now?" Nikki was outraged. "He's the *fuzz*, Crowley! He ain't nothin' but—"

"What he is, Nikki, is someone who's led us to several of your most important missions. Remember those prostitute murders by that vampire with the Jack the Ripper fixation? We wouldn't have known a damn thing about that but for him. Not to mention those nixies in Belvedere Lake, not to mention Darla—"

Holding up a hand even though the gesture was lost over the phone, Nikki said, "All right, all right, I dig it, Crowley, I dig it." She didn't want to hear any more, anyhow, especially if it related to Darla. That lady was a real sore point with Nikki. "But I don't gotta like it."

"I like not knowing about supernatural happenings until it's too late even less. The mission, Nikki—"

"—is what matters, I know. I just got finished telling Robin that."

Robin took that as his cue. "Hi, Mr. Crowley!"

Raising his voice, Crowley said, "Hallo, Robin!"

"He says hi," Nikki said to her son with a little smile. Then back to the phone: "I'm gonna go hit the streets, see what's cookin' this weekend."

"Very well. Keep me posted—we'll meet tonight before you go on patrol."

"You know it. Catch you later."

Nikki hung up the phone and chuckled to herself. Crowley no longer objected to her hitting the streets. He used to, since he thought that the Watchers Council provided him with everything they needed to fight evil, but he soon came around. Her street contacts had proven to be at least as useful as whatever musty old books the Council sent over.

Robin parked himself back in front of the TV—by now *The Lone Ranger* had come on—while Nikki changed into fresh clothes. Someone knocked at the door as she finished tying her platforms.

She opened the door to A.J. Manguson's smiling face. He raised his right hand to his forehead in a mock salute. "Reporting for babysitting duty, ma'am."

Chuckling, Nikki said, "He's all yours, sugar. Thanks."

"No problem," A.J. said as he came in. "Believe me, after dealing with customers all day, a friendly four-year-old's a relief."

From his bedroom, Robin called out, "I'm in here, A.J.! Wanna watch *The Lone Ranger* with me?"

Giving Nikki a pained look, A.J. said, "Great, more Westerns."

"Blame your uncle, don't go blamin' me, Ayj."

Laughing, A.J. said, "Yeah, yeah." He looked over at the bedroom door. "I'll be right there, Rob!"

Nikki put on her leather coat. "Crowley should be here round seven or eight to take over."

"That's cool." A.J. brushed a lock of long blond hair out of his face and gave Nikki a worried look. "Be careful, Nik, okay?"

"Always am, sugar. Thanks again." She headed out the door.

The diner had probably been rather nice when it was first constructed in the 1950s, but twenty years on, Bernard Crowley found it to be a dank, filthy, depressing place—though it was, at least, air-conditioned, providing relief from the heat and humidity outside. Most of the stalls, as well as the counter along one side, were filled with manual laborers, most from the various construction projects that were a near constant in New York even in these poor financial times. As he made his way to the back corner booth, he heard one of them sitting at the counter complain to the waitress behind it about Mayor Beame's work-release program, designed to reduce prison overcrowding by giving convicts honest work.

"Read inna paper that most o' these guys just disappear after they let 'em out."

The waitress shook her head and cracked her gum. "S'crazy, that's what it is."

Bernard had to silently agree. Letting convicted felons out on their own in the hopes that they'd do honest work was as naive—he smiled—as thinking the next Fyarl demon you summoned would be docile.

"Glad you could make it, Bernie."

Sighing, Bernard took the seat opposite Landesberg's in the booth. He had long since given up trying to get the detective to call him something—anything—other than Bernie. "You so rarely call for me in this way, Detective, and when you do, it's usually worth the trip."

Landesberg chuckled. He hadn't changed much in the last four years. His glasses were larger, with black plastic frames, following the style of the day, his curly brown hair had receded a bit, and he'd shaved the mustache after it started showing signs of gray. The remains of a grilled cheese sandwich were on his plate, four butts and one still-lit cigarette were in the ashtray next to him, and he was nursing a cup of coffee that smelled particularly foul.

The waitress had disengaged from her work-release colloquy and walked over. Her hair was in a beehive and frosted within an inch of its life, and she wore enough makeup to qualify as a full face mask. The nameplate on her blouse read DORIS. "Take y'order, hon?"

"Same as his."

Doris nodded, not bothering to write it down. "Grilled cheese and coffee."

"Er, no," he said quickly, "just the sandwich. I'll have a Tab to drink. I'd prefer something cold on this hot day."

"No problem, hon." She cracked her gum. "Cute accent. Where you from?"

"England, originally, though I've lived in New York for the past decade."

Grinning, she said, "Always had a thing for Limeys." With that, she went back behind the counter.

"Charming," Bernard muttered.

Landesberg picked up his cigarette and took a drag. "You get the coffee, you get free refills."

"Hardly an enticement," Bernard said dryly. "Besides, I prefer tea."

"They have tea here."

"No, they have bags of tea dust sitting in puddles of lukewarm water. I'll stick with the soft drink."

"Suit yourself." Landesberg gulped down the rest of his own coffee, set the mug down on the saucer, and said, "Got something that might be up your alley. You know those two women who were killed the other night in the East Village?"

Bernard nodded. "Yes, I recall the news conference. The Fourth Estate wanted very much for this to be another Son of Sam killing, but your commissioner said it was unlikely. He neglected to elaborate, however."

"Yeah, well, they try not to talk about that stuff too much. Anyhow, it wasn't the forty-four killer, that was obvious from the start. Course, the Operation Omega guys are still crawling all over, just in case." He took another drag on his cigarette.

Nodding in sympathy, Bernard said, "Of course." Operation Omega was the task force the NYPD had formed for the express purpose of stopping the Son of Sam, thus far with a distressing lack of results. Indeed, were it not for the fear surrounding the Son of Sam, Bernard doubted that there would have been a news conference for something so—there was, tragically, no other word for it—mundane as the murder of two women.

Doris came back with a can of Tab and a glass full of ice in one hand, and a pot of coffee in the other. She placed the soda in front of Bernard and then refilled Landesberg's cup. Bernard smiled up at her; she cracked her gum again in response.

After she walked away, Landesberg went on. "But no, these two weren't killed with a forty-four—or even with a gun."

"Let me guess," Bernard said, as he pulled the tab off the can and poured its contents into the glass, "they died of exsanguination via puncture wounds in the neck at the carotid artery?"

"How'd you guess?" Landesberg let out a long breath. "I hate this crap, y'know? I like things that make sense. The stuff you and your girl deal with—"

"I can assure you, Detective, that vampires and demons follow a certain pattern and can be stopped if one has the right weapons. I suspect these two young women were simply overpowered by an undead creature whose only way of surviving is to feed upon the living. There's a certain Darwinian simplicity to it— the next link on the food chain, as it were. Vampires kill humans for the same reason that humans kill cows. To my mind, it makes a good deal more sense than a man who shoots people at random with forty-four caliber bullets."

"You got a point." He reached down and pulled a nine-by-twelve manila envelope up from the seat next to him. "Here's a copy of the file."

Bernard hesitated before taking the envelope. "You obtained permission to give me this?"

"Very funny. Maybe if you pulled that Interpol act from four years ago, I coulda done that. Nah, I just snuck into the copy room last night."

"Thank you." Bernard opened the envelope and let the tacky Xerox paper fall out onto the table in front of him.

Before he could look at them, he saw Doris approaching with his sandwich. He quickly piled the papers to the side, placing the envelope on top, covering their contents.

"Grilled cheese for the Limey."

Favoring her with a smile, Bernard said, "Thank you."

"Any time, hon. You need anythin', just holler, okay?"

"Will do."

She turned to Landesberg. "You okay, Artie?"

"Just peachy, Doris."

Satisfied, the waitress beat a retreat, giving Bernard the opportunity to peruse the file.

As he flipped through the pages, Landesberg said, "We don't have much. No sign of forced entry."

"No, they would have had to invite him in first."

"Forensics only got a couple o' useable prints, and they all belonged to the vics." Landesberg leaned back in his seat. "You know what's driving me nuts? They're lookin' for a murder weapon. Coroner said the wounds on their necks are probably bite marks, but nobody's believin' that. And I can't say a damn thing—I got enough of a credibility problem."

At that, Bernard looked up. "You do?"

Smiling wryly, Landesberg said, "Wrong ethnicity. There ain't enough Jews on the force to make a minyan. Hard enough to get taken seriously or get promoted—I start talking about vampires, they park me at a desk and find excuses for me to cash in my pension early. Hell, even if I was Irish or Italian, that'd probably still happen. That's why I go to you."

"Well, I appreciate it. You've been immensely helpful to us."

"So you've said." Landesberg sounded bitter now. "And I guess it is the right thing to do, since none o' the guys I tell you about ever become repeat offenders. But—"

At Landesberg's hesitation, Bernard looked up from the witness statements, which were barely legible, thanks to a poor copy machine and a weak typewriter ribbon. "But what?"

"I took an oath, Bernie."

"As did I. What you're doing right now allows me to fulfill mine so you don't have to break yours."

"How you figure that?"

Bernard set down the papers. "The NYPD is barely able to handle the crimes it was designed to solve. The prisons are so overcrowded the mayor's releasing inmates, there's a killer on the loose that no one can find, and from what one reads in the papers, your negotiations with the city are not going well."

Landesberg shrugged as he took a final drag on his cigarette and then stubbed it out in the ashtray with the others. "That's just the usual union garbage."

"Yes, usual—and you're barely handling it. You're

not equipped to fight vampires or werewolves or demons. The Slayer, however, is. For centuries, the Slayers have been tasked with protecting humanity from creatures so foul that they can't ever know about them. This city is in a poor enough condition at the moment—do you really think a populace that is paralyzed with fear over the Son of Sam, crippled by poverty and joblessness, and hamstrung by poor civil services is ready to find out that there are vampires preying on them?"

Snorting, Landesberg said, "Hell, *I'm* not ready to find out, and I figured it out three years ago when your girl was around for half the NYPD's open cases."

Bernard looked back down at the file. Nikki had generally been good about covering her tracks. Indeed, had Landesberg not been the detective in charge of Nikki's grandmother's murder investigation, with its talk of vampires, he might not have made the connection in the first place.

But make it he had. In truth, Bernard was grateful, both that he did figure it out, and that his place in the NYPD was sufficiently insecure to prevent him from telling his superiors. Bernard suspected that the latter had more to do with Landesberg's lack of political skills than his ethnicity, but either way, it benefited Bernard and Nikki to have someone on the force who believed in what they did and gave them the chance to take care of it before any of the constabulary got hurt.

"Oh, one other thing—we got a possible description. Last place the girls were seen alive was CBGB's, and the bartender saw them going out with someone. Sketch artist did a doodle—it's at the bottom of the file."

Nodding, Bernard riffled through the papers until he got to the sketch.

When he saw the face, he almost dropped his soda glass.

"What is it?" Landesberg asked.

"Nothing—just thought I recognized the chap for a second."

"You know who he is?"

"Not at all—just reminds me of someone I knew back in England. Couldn't be the same fellow."

Bernard had no idea if Landesberg believed him, but at the moment he didn't care. If this sketch was accurate, Nikki was in serious trouble.

Because if the witness who gave the artist the description was to be believed, William the Bloody was in town.

Nikki walked confidently up Tenth Avenue, her leather coat billowing behind her. She wore a light cotton T-shirt under it so she wouldn't be completely sweaty in the eighty-plus-degree temps and crappy humidity. But she *had* to wear the coat. Without it, she was just some chick walkin' down the street.

With it, she was the Slayer, and nobody messed with her. At least, they didn't twice.

Usually folks just crowded past one another when they walked down the street, but as soon as they saw Nikki, they got out of her way. Even people who didn't know her, knew better than to get too close to her. She was *dangerous*.

And that was how she liked it.

A little kid ran up to her. "What's happenin', Big Mamma Jamma?"

Grinning, Nikki stopped walking and knelt down to look him in the eye. The boy's name was Hank, and his aunt and uncle ran a small delicatessen on Tenth Avenue and 45th Street. Hank, who was only twelve, helped out in the store, and he heard things and sometimes passed them on to Nikki. Of course, like most of her contacts, he didn't know Nikki's name; that was why he used the nickname, which was straight out of *Cleopatra Jones*.

"Not much, little man," she said. "You got somethin' for me?"

"Yeah—those mean fangy dudes're shakin' down my uncle's store again."

Nikki frowned. Despite her warnings to his henchvamps, Reet was still trying to expand his protection racket, using bloodsuckers to force people to pay up or get their places of business trashed. "They say when they comin' back to collect?"

"Tonight—'bout nine thirty."

She put her hands on Hank's shoulders. "Sugar, I want you to go and tell your aunt and uncle that they don't gotta pay nothin', you dig? The Slayer'll take care of it."

Hank broke into a huge grin. "Outta sight!"

"You know it."

"Hey, can I ask you somethin'?"

Nodding, Nikki said, "Sure."

"You ever meet Dracula?"

At that, Nikki had to laugh. "Yeah, I met that fool once. 'Bout two years ago now."

Hank's eyes went all wide. "Fool? But Count Dracula's the baddest mother on the block! You ever seen his movies?"

"Yeah, I seen 'em. Movies ain't real life, and the real Drac ain't got nothin' on William Marshall." She stood up and held out a hand, palm up. "Now gimme five."

He slapped her palm with his. "Right on, Big Mamma Jamma!" Then he ran off.

As Nikki continued down the street, she put thoughts of Dracula out of her mind. Reet was her main problem. Nikki had been the Slayer for four years now; Reet and Dracula were two of the only three bloodsuckers she hadn't been able to take care of for good. She'd chipped away at Reet's organization, dusted a ton of his boys, messed up a whole lot of his schemes, and saved a lot of people he might have killed otherwise, but in the end, Reet was still the main man in Harlem, and there wasn't a damn thing Nikki could do about it.

She even knew where he was most of the time: That damn building on Lenox, right around the corner from the apartment where she and Robin used to live with Gramma. But the place had tighter security than Fort Knox, plus half the fuzz in Harlem was on Reet's payroll—he practically owned the damn 28th Precinct. She got anywhere near the building, she'd be under arrest in no time flat. The mission was what mattered, and she couldn't do the mission if she was in jail—or if she was a fugitive who broke out of Rikers Island or Sing Sing or wherever they'd send her.

So Reet's HQ was off-limits. That just left his racket, and Nikki could *damn* well do damage there.

However, she wouldn't need to set up at the deli until after sunset, which wouldn't be for a couple of hours, so Nikki kept walking until she reached the large newsstand on the corner of 44th Street. This late in the day, there weren't very many newspapers left. The *Times* was all gone, but there were still a few copies of the *Daily News* and the *Post*.

Sitting in his usual spot on the stool in front of the newsstand, leaning thoughtfully on his cane, was Blind Willie, his Seeing Eye dog, Bartholomew, lying down on the pavement at his side, eyes closed. Willie wore the same army fatigues he always wore—he told Nikki once that he had joined the army so he wouldn't have to figure out what to wear every day—but he'd taken the button-down shirt off because of the weather, just sitting in the green undershirt smoking a cigarette. Creeping out from under his large sunglasses, some scarring could be seen on his face, courtesy of a grenade that went off near him in Korea. He used the money he got from the army to buy this newsstand, and he'd been running it ever since, becoming a fixture in a neighborhood he'd never again be able to see.

But he made up for it with what he heard.

"What's happenin', Willie?"

"Good to hear your voice, baby girl," Willie said, still staring sightlessly straight ahead.

Nikki reached into her pocket and pulled out two dimes, dropping them into the dish that sat on the ledge of the newsstand next to the candy bars, right in Willie's reach, and grabbing the last copy of the *Daily News*. "Good to see you, sugar. You hear anythin'?"

"Lotsa things. Martha Johnson's oldest got himself a scholarship to Morehouse down in Atlanta—but he's goin' to John Jay instead. Wants to become *po*lice."

Nikki gave a snort to that.

Willie took a drag on his cigarette. "Yeah, I hear you, baby girl, but that boy's stubborn as a mule. Can't see what's good for him."

"It's a shame. Last thing we need's more fuzz."

"I heard that." Willie nodded. A teenage girl walked by, grabbed a *Post*, dropped coins in the bowl, and moved on without even acknowledging Willie or Nikki. The vendor went on, "Hank's worried about his uncle's deli."

"Yeah, I already talked to him. I'm on it."

"Good to hear, baby girl, good to hear. Lessee, what else?"

Nikki tucked the paper under her arm and waited patiently. Willie generally took a long and winding road to his point, but he got there eventually. Nikki figured he just liked having someone to talk to—most folks just talked at him all the time, or didn't even know he was there, like that girl just now—and she was willing to be his listener, long as he eventually gave her something she could use.

"The Sookdars are havin' another baby—that makes, what, seven? Gonna get mighty crowded in that pad o' theirs." He finished his cigarette, dropped it onto the pavement, stepped on it, pulled another out of his camo pants pocket, and lit it. "And then there's a new girl workin' Forty-ninth and Eleventh—takin' Miranda's place. Only, from what I hear tell, she ain't no she, you dig? She's a whatcha call—transvestiture."

"Transvestite, actually." Nikki didn't have much schooling, but she knew enough.

"Whatever you call it, Sue was complainin' that he's better-lookin' than her."

"Don't take much." Sue was a hooker, and she was almost the fourth victim of that vampire who had been trying to be the second coming of Jack the Ripper. The street life had not been kind to her face, which Nikki didn't think was much to begin with.

"Oh, and I heard there was a new vamp on the scene."

Finally. Blind Willie knew all about vampires and such. He didn't know her name or where she lived, either, but somehow he knew about Slayers already—he said something happened in the war but never gave specifics—and passed on anything he heard to her. He didn't have info for her very often, but when he did, it was always a good tip, even if it usually took him half an hour to get there.

Willie added, "Ain't one o' Reet's, neither. He's English."

"English, huh? He black or white?"

Grinning, Willie asked, "They got black folks over there?"

Shuddering, Nikki thought back to her cruciamentum, a brutal trial by fire that the Watchers threw at her on her eighteenth birthday. She'd met several of Crowley's fellow Watchers on that awful day, all of them as British as Crowley, and one of them was a brother. Not that she'd willingly call *any* of them "brother" after what they did to her. That was another reason why she preferred to rely on the streets instead of Crowley's people for info.

"Yeah, a few."

"Well, this ain't one of 'em. He one o' them punk honkies like they got there."

Rubbing her chin, Nikki asked, "You sure he ain't one o' Reet's? I wouldn't put it past him to bring in foreign muscle."

"Nah, I know he ain't, on account o' it's Reet's folks I found out from. They lookin' for him."

Nikki nodded. That fit Reet's MO—if there was a new bloodsucker in town, that vamp got either recruited or staked.

"Right on, Willie, thanks. I'll keep an eye out for this punk British honky bloodsucker dude."

"You do that, baby girl. And you're welcome."

Nikki reached into her pocket and pulled out a dollar bill to toss into the bowl.

Willie shook his head and started petting Bartholomew with the hand that wasn't holding the cigarette. "You don't gotta be doin' that, baby girl. You don't owe me nothin'."

"Ain't about owin', Willie. Thanks."

She headed over to the phone booth on the corner. Crowley was probably still with that cop pal of his, but she could leave a message with A.J. After being reassured that Robin was okay, she said that she'd be remonstrating with some bad guys tonight and would therefore be home late. A.J. assured her he'd pass on the message.

That done, she headed toward Tenth and 45th. She had a couple of henchvamps to get out of the protection racket.

Chapter Seven

**New York City
July 8, 1977
9:45 p.m.**

From his vantage point on the filthy rooftop across West 45th Street, Spike watched the Slayer in action.

This was Spike's first trip back to the Yank side of the pond since Woodstock eight years past, and his first time back in the city proper in a lot longer than that. He had to admit to being pretty disgusted with the filth. True, the streets of urban England in the late nineteenth century, where he'd spent his human life, weren't models of cleanliness, but they also had lower standards then. There was no reason for there to be so much garbage around in the late twentieth century. The heat and humidity didn't help—the tar on the roof was halfway to a liquid, even with the sun having gone down, and Spike's black boots were sinking into it.

But that wasn't Spike's primary concern—rather, it was the girl in the alleyway on 45th a few meters in from Tenth Avenue, behind a chip shop of some sort, beating the living daylights out of two of Spike's fellow vampires.

Girl, hell—that's a full-blown woman, that is. The most recent Slayer had, by the looks of her, made it into her twenties, which was no small feat. Most Slayers didn't live to twenty-five.

The two vampires were of the standard big-and-stupid variety. In fact, Spike had dubbed them Big and Stupid. Right now, Big was trying to grab the Slayer, but she ducked under his lunge so fast her coat flapped up into Big's face. Then she kicked him hard with her outsize shoe right in the knee.

While Big hobbled about, Stupid got up from the Dumpster the Slayer had tossed him onto and jumped on top of her. The Slayer rolled with it and they both crashed into a metal garbage can. Stupid recovered faster and picked up the garbage can, holding it over his head as if to slam it down on her.

That trick never works, Spike thought, shaking his head. The biggest flaw with most vampires, and Spike had to admit to being guilty of it himself all too often, was theatrics. It was one thing if you were good at it, like Angelus—whatever Spike thought of his grandsire, the old bastard knew how to stage a beautiful killing—but when you were just some ponce with fangs, it was more often not worth the effort.

Case in point: If Stupid had just stepped on the Slayer's face, the fight would be finished, but no, he had to go and show off by hefting the sodding can.

Result? The Slayer had plenty of time to kick Stupid in his goolies, causing him to lose his grip on the can, which then came crashing onto the vampire's own head.

Out of the blue, Spike wondered how Angelus was doing. He hadn't seen the Irish vamp since that to-do on the German U-boat during the war. Not that Spike missed him overmuch. Best thing that ever happened to him and Dru was to cut themselves off from Darla and Angelus back in China. Both of them had been acting bloody peculiar in any case.

Besides, that had been when Spike bagged his first Slayer.

Best day of his life, that was, and he'd been trying to reexperience it ever since. It had been just shy of a century past when Angelus had first told him about the Slayer, the girl chosen to be the killer of vampires and demons and things that go biggledy-boggledy in the night. Took two decades, but Spike had finally come across one during the Boxer Rebellion. Spike, Dru, and Darla had gone to Peking at the latter's request. Religious insurgency always got the old witch's blood boiling, and Dru and Spike went along for kicks. Angelus, who'd gone AWOL since they'd massacred that gypsy tribe two years earlier, had finally turned up to join them as well.

After Spike had taken down that Slayer, though, Angelus had disappeared, and Darla had soon followed—leaving Spike and Dru free to roam and find more Slayers to kill.

But it hadn't happened. Oh, Spike had found plenty of Slayers, but half of them had died by the time he was able to catch up to them, and the rest had managed to beat him back. There was one occasion when he and Dru, at the behest of a demon, killed a whole pack of potential Slayers to winnow the field, as it were. And other times he had been distracted with more entertaining matters. Fact was, he hadn't gone on a serious Slayer hunt since the fifties.

Now, though, he had time on his hands. He and Dru had had yet another row. Most of the time, Spike could handle Dru's eccentricity, but sometimes it got to be too much, and he'd lose it. He generally regretted his fits of temper, but Dru wasn't always so forgiving. This particular time—right after they had massacred an entire theater company in Paris—she had reminded him that she had only made him as a plaything for herself, and that meant he should do as she said.

Spike hadn't taken kindly to that. He was his own man, not some bint's plaything, even if that bint was the vampire he loved.

So he had buggered off to England, found himself a Watcher to intimidate, and learned everything he could about the most recent Slayer.

The Watcher had only given him a name (Nikki Wood), a location (New York City), and a phone number for the answering service used by the girl's

Watcher. One steamer ride to New York Harbor later, and he was on the case.

To his surprise, in the days since his arrival, and despite his refreshing meal after CBGB's, he had actually learned *less* than he had gotten from that weed of a Watcher. All the usual sources for demonic info knew only that there was a Slayer in town, and the smart vampire didn't mess with her. Nobody even knew her name.

Stupid was dazed on the litter-strewn pavement, leaving Big to try another grab, which was about as successful as the first one. *I'm thinking I got the nicknames backward,* Spike thought. This time Big managed to grab the coat, at least, but the Slayer still kicked him, this time in the stomach.

She also spoke for the first time. "Hands *off* the coat, turkey!"

Spike smiled. He didn't blame her for being protective—that was a *fine* coat she wore.

Nikki punched Big a few more times, ending with a haymaker that sent Big crashing into the Dumpster. *A haymaker—amazing.* Spike had seen over half a dozen Slayers in the last seventy-seven years. Until this one, they all had evidence of Oriental martial arts training. The girl in China was the most impressive—she was like a dancer, waving that enchanted sword around. Vampiric healing notwithstanding, Spike still had the cut on his eyebrow from that blade, which was why he assumed the sword to have been enchanted. In retrospect, he should have found out what had been done to that weapon, but he was young then.

But where that girl, and all the other Slayers he'd seen, looked like Bruce Lee, this one fought more like Muhammad Ali. She didn't have the elegance Spike had come to associate with Slayers—she was more of a pugilist, hacking and punching and kicking her way to success.

Then the Slayer pulled her stake out of one of the leather coat's pockets and threw it across the alley at Big.

It hit his heart dead-on, and Big collapsed into dust.

She then walked over to Stupid, who was still rolling on the ground clutching his groin. *Soddin' hell,* Spike thought at Stupid, *be a man.*

Nikki picked Stupid up by the fringe-covered vest that was all the vampire was wearing above the waist, apart from the bandanna around his head.

"Ain't gonna kill you, Hodge. Got a message for Reet, and I want *you* to deliver it. You tell that turkey to keep away from Hell's Kitchen. He got Harlem already, he is *not* expandin' his racket. You hearin' me, fool?"

"You're—you're lettin' me go?"

Smiling, Nikki said, "You gonna deliver the message?"

Nodding quickly, Stupid—or, rather, Hodge—said, "Right on, sister, I'll deliver any message you want, long as you ain't stakin' me."

"Cool." The Slayer let go of Hodge, and he fell to the pavement, then quickly scrambled to his feet and ran out of the alley and down 45th, across Tenth, and on toward Ninth.

Spike nodded. *Not bad. Good job to scope her out first. Would've approached this all wrong and bollixed it up.* Nikki didn't have the intricacy of the other Slayers, but he realized that there was still a brutal elegance about her style. However, she wasn't a finesse fighter, so Spike would have to adjust accordingly.

The other adjustment was in how Nikki operated. Usually Slayers were under the radar. Nobody knew she was there, except for the demons she killed, her Watcher, and damn few others.

But, while most of the so-called Big Apple was as oblivious as the rest of the world to the presence of vampires, there were some who knew that there was a Slayer looking out for them. Most of them were in Hell's Kitchen, Times Square, and Harlem, where people were talking up the Slayer like she was the second coming of Malcolm bloody X.

Irritatingly, none of the meat puppets had given up anything either. While this Slayer wasn't as covert as her predecessors, she was just as secretive—she simply did it by going all folk hero. Which didn't really help him narrow down where she might live.

The stories they had told him were a bit outlandish, as well. One bloke told him that the Slayer was the one who stopped the city from tearing down Grand Central Terminal. Another said the Slayer stopped the apocalypse from happening during the bicentennial (as if the two hundredth anniversary of this colony-with-delusions would be worth marking with an apocalypse, Spike had thought disdainfully). Then there were the tots who assured Spike that the

Slayer made their mama and their papa get back together. Spike's favorite was the bird who confidently stated that the Slayer was really the Son of Sam killer, and that all her victims were really vampires in disguise.

The only useful intelligence Spike had received was word that the Slayer planned to take out some bloodsuckers that were extracting protection money from a deli on 45th and Tenth. Spike had viewed that as an ideal opportunity to do some reconnaissance.

He watched as Nikki went into the store—no doubt to assure the owners that she'd taken care of business—and then he got up and ran across the dirty roof to the fire escape on the other side. It was getting late, and the Ramones would be starting soon. *I didn't spend two weeks in a cargo hold just to miss the bloody Ramones. . . .*

Tomorrow night he'd start the dance with Nikki the Vampire Slayer.

Chapter Eight

New York City
July 8, 1977
10:15 p.m.

Nikki walked up the creaky stairs to her apartment in a fine mood. She'd gotten to stake Bodie and scare his sidekick Hodge half to death. Hodge'd deliver the message to Reet, and Reet'd probably stake him on general principles anyhow. She'd crossed paths with Bodie and Hodge a few times in the last month or so, and she was glad to be rid of them. They weren't Commies, which disappointed Marty when she told him about it on the way inside the theater, but she was completely cool with it.

The Gem was showing *The Good, the Bad, and the Ugly*, so it was with the muffled voice of Clint Eastwood as the Man with No Name reverberating through the walls that Nikki entered her apartment.

She found Crowley sitting on the couch, reading one of his dusty old books and smoking a cigarette. More books sat in a pile on the crate next to the pottery ashtray, which was full of cigarette butts. "You know, Crowley, I got enough funky smells in this pad without you bringin' your library down."

Crowley looked up, only just registering that Nikki had come in. "Hmm? Oh, sorry, Nikki, I was caught up. Don't worry, Robin's already fast asleep, despite the cinematic nonsense."

Since it was two hours after Robin's bedtime, Nikki for damn sure hoped he was in bed. She tossed her coat onto the easy chair, then sat down while she unlaced her platforms. "Sorry for stayin' out late, but—"

"Yes, young Mr. Manguson passed on your message. I take it that Reet is trying to expand his protection racket?"

"Tryin' and failin'," she said as she kicked off her shoes. "I dusted Bodie and sent Hodge back with a note from Big Mama Slayer."

"Well done," Crowley said quickly, "but I'm afraid that we have bigger fish to fry. Two, to be precise. First of all, I received a message from the Council. Apparently, tomorrow at sunset is the commencement of the Feast of Pohldak. I would've sworn that it wasn't for a few more months, but there it is."

"So what happens on the Feast of Pohldak?" Nikki asked as she stretched her arms, feeling the bones in her neck and shoulders snap, crackle, and pop.

"Thankfully, not much, but certain magical hot spots become a good deal more—well, fertile. From what the Council said in their message, Sheep Meadow will be one of the big ones, so it's quite likely that some miscreant will be trying to raise a demon or cast a spell or some such there. Best if you keep an eye on it."

Nikki leaned back in the chair, her Afro settling against the leather coat. "That works out fine. I was gonna take Robin to one o' the zoos tomorrow. It'll just be the Central Park one, and I'll swing by Sheep Meadow round sunset."

Crowley winced. "You may not want to endanger Robin—"

Rolling her eyes, Nikki said, "You said it would just be some miscreants. It ain't a major ritual thing, right?"

"No, but . . ." Crowley grabbed his cigarette and took a drag.

When Crowley's hesitation went on way too long, Nikki said, "But what?"

"I'm less concerned about Pohldak than I am about the second fish that needs frying. You see, there's a new vampire in town."

Figures Crowley heard about this too. "British honky punk, right?"

Crowley blinked a few times. "Er, well, yes."

Nikki chuckled at Crowley's surprise. "Blind Willie told me 'bout him. Said Reet's boys're lookin' for him—prob'ly to recruit."

"Yes, well, that's unlikely."

Not liking the tone in Crowley's voice, Nikki leaned forward again. "What's goin' on, Crowley? Who is this cat?"

Crowley set the book down and got up from the couch. He started pacing the small room, puffing on his cigarette, finally stopping at the window that looked out over 42nd Street. "The vampire is called William the Bloody, sometimes known by the nom du guerre of 'Spike.' Apparently, he used to delight in torturing victims by driving railroad spikes through their heads."

Shrugging, Nikki said, "So he's a regular nasty bloodsucker. I'll stake his ass like I would any—"

"He's *not* just a regular nasty bloodsucker, Nikki," Crowley snapped, whirling on her. "I've brought these books here because they include what we know about William—and his cohorts."

Nikki didn't like the sound of that, either. "What cohorts?"

"William is often in the company of a vampire called Drusilla. They seem to be lovers—where William is sadistic, Drusilla is quite mad. She's also rumored to have precognition."

"What kinda disease is that?"

That actually got a smile out of Crowley. "It's not a disease, Nikki, it means she can see the future."

She leaned back again. "Great. Look, I did my good deed tonight, and I'm feelin' cool. We gotta do this now?"

"I'm afraid we must—you see, Nikki, William's other two known associates are a vicious killer named Angelus—and Darla."

Suddenly Nikki shot out of the easy chair. "What?"

Crowley was still standing by the window, now running his free hand over his bald head while holding the cigarette in the other. "In the late nineteenth century, Angelus, William, Drusilla, *and* Darla cut a swath through Europe and Asia. They began in London in 1880, worked their way through the continent and later the Balkans, and eventually wound up in China during the Boxer Rebellion in 1900. As it happens, the current Slayer was in Peking at the time." Up until now, Crowley had been studying the floor while he talked, but he looked up to tell her this: "She fought William, and he killed her."

However, Nikki was focused on a different part of the conversation. "This William cat—he ran with Darla?"

"Yes." Crowley nodded slowly. "But, to be honest, the last report of the four of them seen together was from Peking, seventy-seven years ago."

Nikki started pacing. "Yeah, but for all we know, they're bosom buddies. Dammit, Crowley, we gotta—"

Crowley put his free hand on her shoulder, causing her to raise her arms defensively before she forced herself to put them down. To his credit, Crowley didn't flinch, trusting his Slayer.

Wish I trusted myself that much, Nikki thought. *I can't believe that bitch might be back.*

"I've put in a call to the Council already," Crowley said calmly, "and according to their most recent intelligence, Darla is still in Italy. They're checking again, and we should know tomorrow sometime."

"Sooner the better, Crowley—if that bitch is back, I want to *know*."

For the last year, Nikki had been going over what happened with Darla, and every time it came back to the same missed chance. They'd fought several times, including a donnybrook that almost tore Studio 54 apart, but Nikki hadn't been able to defeat the vampire. Every time, Darla managed to distract Nikki or sneak out or do *some* damn thing.

The final straw was when Nikki had chased the blond bitch to the 79th Street Boat Basin. Nikki had arrived just a minute too late—Darla's boat was pulling into the Hudson River. The vampire had set all the other boats in the basin on fire, leaving Nikki standing impotently amid the flames, holding a stake that she couldn't do a damn thing with.

It was after that encounter that she started practicing throwing her stake. She spent months getting that down to the point where she'd nailed a dozen bloodsuckers that way, including Bodie tonight. She wasn't getting caught out like *that* again.

Suddenly something Crowley had said finally registered. "He killed a Slayer, you said?"

Crowley nodded. "At the turn of the century in Peking. Spike has encountered a few others as well, though he's only killed the one. According to one report, he's rather obsessed on the subject of Slayers." He looked away. "And if he's brought either Drusilla or Darla or Angelus or any combination of them . . ." He looked back at her. "These next few days will be difficult."

"Yeah, well, difficult was when those Polgara demons stomped through Fordham University. Difficult was when those six vampires fed between games of a doubleheader at Shea. Difficult—"

Holding up a hand, Crowley said, "I get the idea. Still, we'll need to plan. For one thing . . ." He let out a smoky breath. "William, Angelus, Darla, Drusilla—they all have a tendency to take over whatever group of vampires they're in. So don't be surprised if William tries to move in on Reet's territory. My fear is that he's *not* alone. Angelus is one of the most vicious killers the world has ever known, Drusilla's a madwoman, William has killed a Slayer—and you know about Darla." Once again he put a hand on her shoulder. "Yes, you've faced difficulties in the past, but this has the potential to be the worst."

Nikki nodded, then shrugged off Crowley's hand and walked over to the easy chair. She picked up her coat and slung it over her shoulders, shrugging into it. "Then I'd best be gettin' my black ass back out there."

"Indeed," Crowley said. "And watch that ass, Miss Wood."

That got Nikki's attention. The music from *The Good, the Bad, and the Ugly* filtered through the walls just as she put her hand on the doorknob.

Crowley only called her "Miss Wood" when he wanted to get her attention.

"I will," she said.

"Oh, one more thing." Crowley walked over to the couch and picked up a manila envelope that Nikki hadn't noticed. He pulled a sheet of paper out and showed it to Nikki. "This is what William looks like."

Nikki peered at the piece of paper, which was a black-and-white pencil drawing of a dude with spiky hair—*that fits with his nickname*—and a scar on his left eyebrow. "Thought bloodsuckers didn't scar."

"Oh, they do, they just usually heal." Crowley put out his cigarette. "It's the legacy William carries from his victory over your Asian predecessor. She carried an enchanted sword—a gift from a Buddhist monk she rescued from a dragon once—and used it on William. He's carried the scar ever since."

Looking around her apartment, which was also a gift from a grateful rescuee, Nikki wondered who'd gotten the better end of the deal. *Enchanted sword would come in real handy right now.*

Then she rejected the notion. Cleopatra Jones and Batman didn't use swords, either.

Giving Crowley a nod, she went out on patrol. Right now, more than anything, Nikki was in the mood to hit something.

Chapter Nine

New York City
July 9, 1977
8:45 p.m.

Robin kept insisting it wasn't going to rain, but Nikki made him take a rain slicker and galoshes anyway when they went to Central Park. Robin said it wasn't fair, it *wasn't* going to rain, and Mama was just being silly.

But Nikki wouldn't take no for an answer. She wasn't about to let her baby boy catch a cold. And if it didn't rain, then Robin got exercise carrying around the little bag with the boots and coat, so he could be big and strong like Mama.

That usually got Robin to stop complaining. At least for a little while.

Patrol hadn't gone all that well the previous night. She'd stopped a couple more vamps from pulling the same garbage on an auto parts place uptown that Bodie and Hodge were pulling on Hank's aunt and uncle's deli. But otherwise, Nikki was distracted. This William dude sounded like bad news, and if Darla was with him . . .

In four years of slaying, the worst feeling Nikki had ever had was standing there on the boat basin, stake clutched in her hand, boats burning around her, and feeling completely helpless while Darla sailed away. Nikki had come *this close* to jumping in the water after her, but Nikki didn't know how to swim, and even if she did, diving into the Hudson River was taking your life into your hands.

So she had just stood there.

Now she was standing outside the carousel, watching Robin bob up and down on a white horse, laughing and having a great time.

Thoughts of Darla and this William the Bloody cat fell out of her head—or at least moved to the back of it—and she laughed as she watched her baby boy holding on to the golden pole and saying, "Hi-Yo, Silver—*away!*" as he passed by Nikki, just like the Lone Ranger did on TV.

When the carousel slowed to a stop, Robin joined the other children running around the black fence until they reached the EXIT sign. Nikki was waiting for him on the other side.

"Didja see, Mama? I caught the outlaws!"

Getting down on her knees, Nikki smiled. "Good job, baby boy! You gonna take 'em to jail?"

"Nah, Tonto'll do that. I had to come back to you!"

Chuckling, Nikki got to her feet, took Robin's hand, and started walking toward the Sheep Meadow.

It had been a good day, for the most part. At first Robin had been disappointed that they weren't going to the Bronx Zoo—he really had his heart set on Wild Asia—but Nikki said maybe next weekend. Mama had to check something in Central Park for Crowley at sunset, she said. By the time they took the IRT up to the Bronx Zoo and back again, it would be too late. "The mission," she had reminded him, "is what matters." Then she had smiled. "Besides, we can go on the carousel!"

Robin had always loved the carousel.

Still, even as they looked at giraffes and zebras and lions and penguins and monkeys, Nikki's mind had been wandering. Robin pointing excitedly at some animal or other had usually been enough to drag her back to the present, but then she'd find herself mentally back on that damn boat basin, clutching the stake.

Or she'd be thinking about a Slayer in Peking in 1900, and the fact that the vamp who had killed that girl was now stalking Nikki.

She was used to being a target. Every bloodsucker in the city wanted a piece of her, and every one of them would've loved to be able to make the same claim as this William cat—that they iced a Slayer. But that was because Nikki had been spending four years making their lives miserable.

But William the Bloody had come to New York just so he could kill Nikki Wood—or, more to the point, kill the Slayer. It wasn't because she'd messed with his rackets or kept him from feeding. She was cool with cats who wanted to kill her because of what she'd done.

It was being killed because of who she was that didn't sit right with her.

"Mama, you okay?"

Nikki blinked, then looked down at Robin's big brown eyes. "I'm fine, baby boy."

"You don't seem fine."

Chuckling, Nikki said, "Sorry, Robin. Mama's just distracted, that's all."

"What's Crowley need you to do?"

"There might be somethin' goin' down in Sheep Meadow at sunset." Nikki looked up. It was getting dark awfully fast. Sure enough, dark clouds were starting to move in.

The carousel was right on one corner of Sheep Meadow, which was pretty big, so Nikki and Robin wandered around it. At Nikki's prompting, Robin started explaining about the outlaws he'd been chasing on the carousel. Apparently, they were tiger rustlers, who'd stolen tigers from the zoo, and it was up to the Lone Ranger—Robin—and Tonto to get them back. The outlaws had really fast horses, but Silver was faster than any of them, and Robin got the bad guys.

Nikki heard every word Robin said, and she nodded occasionally or said, "Outta sight" or "Right on" to acknowledge his accomplishments in stopping the evil tiger rustlers, but she was also watching the people in Sheep Meadow. Over here, some kids smoking joints. Over there, two hippie cats playing acoustic guitars and singing off-key to an audience of about a dozen people with hair just as long. Several hot dog stands, all with lines. Sunbathers, most of whom were packing it in now that the light was going away. Kids throwing Frisbees around. A brother playing fetch with a big golden retriever.

But nobody who looked like they were performing magical rituals. Nikki had been doing this long enough to recognize the signs, even when folks were trying to hide what they were doing, but the people in the Meadow today were just out to be cool.

Then it got even darker. "Robin, honey, put your galoshes on."

"But Mama—"

"Do what I say, Robin," Nikki said, even as the first drop hit her on the face with a mild splash.

By the time Robin had climbed into his galoshes and put his raincoat on, it was pouring. Most of the people in the Meadow had scattered, and Robin and Nikki were doing the same, heading northwest toward the 72nd Street transverse. They'd catch the CC train there, take it back to the Gem. By the time they reached the paved walkway that would lead them to the transverse, it was pitch-dark out.

So Nikki shouldn't have been entirely surprised when a vampire jumped her.

And after she managed to knock the vampire to the ground, she was even less surprised to recognize the face that looked up from the wet pavement at her, illuminated by the lightning that sizzled through the air.

William the Bloody, aka Spike.

He wore a leather jacket over a ripped black T-shirt, dungarees with a hole in the left knee, and metal studs all over. He even wore a chain around his neck with a small gold padlock on it. She saw the scar over his left eye where he'd been cut by the enchanted sword, and again Nikki found herself thinking it might come in handy.

Hell with that—didn't do her any good, neither.

Out of the corner of her eye, Nikki saw that Robin had run to hide behind a park bench. *Good boy, Robin.* Although she did what she could to avoid it, this wasn't the first time she'd gotten sucked into a fight when Robin was around—and even if it had been, they'd practiced what to do in case Nikki was attacked when they were together—and her baby boy knew to stay hidden until it was safe.

"Let's get this over with, shall we, Slayer? My name's Spike, and I've come to kill you."

"Pleased to meet you," she said as she punched him. Then she turned and cartwheeled, kicking him twice in the face. Whirling around, she found that Spike had gotten back to his feet very quickly. He had his game face on now, and he was grinning like a fool.

"Well, all *right*—you got the moves, don't you? I'm gonna ride you hard before I put *you* away, love."

"You sure about that? You actually look a little wet and limp to me." She smiled. "And I ain't your 'love.'" Then she attacked, kicking him again.

He returned with a kick of his own. They sparred back and forth for a minute—this Spike dude was *incredibly* fast, and a lot stronger than most of the bloodsuckers she'd tangled with.

Somehow, he knocked her down. Her coat protected her from the wet pavement, at least, but the rain pelted down on her face. Spike straddled her and started whaling on her—he got two punches to her face before she managed to get her left arm up to block the third one.

That surprised him enough to make him hesitate; she hit him, then bent her knees and kicked him in the stomach with both feet.

She didn't let up her assault, because she knew she couldn't afford to. This wasn't one of Reet's turkeys. Spike knew his business, and Nikki had to keep punching and kicking if she was going to win this fight.

Moving faster than Nikki thought was possible, Spike managed to grab her right arm as she tried to punch him in the face. Then he yanked it down and turned her around, pinning both arms.

Spike was standing behind her, and she could feel his hot breath on her neck. She struggled but simply could not move her arms.

A garbage can fell over. Spike hesitated.

Nikki took advantage, slamming her head back into his face, for once regretting her Afro, as it blunted the blow. Still, it was enough to get Spike to let go. She elbowed him in the stomach, then grabbed his left arm and flipped him over, sending him tumbling down the rain-soaked walkway.

Time to end this. She pulled out her stake and threw it unerringly at Spike's heart just as he got up.

And he caught it.

Agape, Nikki stared at him. For nine months, ever since she'd perfected the move, she'd been tossing stakes at vamps and killing them. She hadn't failed to dust one that way yet.

Until today. Spike reached up and slapped his palms on either side of the stake, stopping it short of his heart. It was like he'd been expecting it.

Spike grinned, still holding the stake. "I spent a long time trying to track you down. Never really want the dance to end so soon, do you—Nikki? Music's just started, innit?"

A fist of ice clenched Nikki's heart.

He knows my name.

Spike tossed the stake to the ground, then jumped up onto one of the knee-high brick walls that bordered the walkway and kept pedestrians from falling down the incline on the other side of it.

"By the way," he said with a big grin, "*love* the coat."

And then he was gone.

He knows my name.

"Mama?"

Nikki whirled around to see Robin coming out from behind the bench. Then she turned back to look at where Spike had been standing a moment before.

The son of a bitch knows my name.

For four years, the way she'd kept Robin safe was to never let anyone know who she was. All anybody knew was that she was the Slayer.

Until now. This vampire—who'd already killed one Slayer—knew her name.

What else does he know?

She walked over to her son, still standing next to the concrete-and-wood bench, and knelt down so she was face-to-face with him. The rain was running in rivulets down her face, but she didn't care. She said, "You did a good job, baby boy. You stayed down, just like Mama told you."

"Can we go home now?" Gone was the excited little boy talking about how he and Tonto stopped the evil tiger rustlers. Now Robin Wood was just a scared four-year-old boy.

Much as it pained Nikki, though, home was no longer an option. If Spike was looking for her, it meant he knew where to find a Slayer. He probably knew about the Pohldak thing, and so he was lurking in the park.

And he knows my name. So he might know where I live.

Shaking her head, she replied, "Nuh-uh—it's not safe there anymore. How 'bout I leave you over Crowley's house? You can play with those spooky doodads you like." She smiled, trying to put a good face on it. Of course, most of Crowley's doodads weren't safe for Robin to play with, but the Watcher had a bunch of child-safe ones he let Robin fool around with when he was there.

However, her baby boy wasn't gonna be bribed by magic. "No, I wanna stay with you."

"Yeah, I know you do, baby." Nikki sighed. This conversation was breaking her heart. "But remember, Robin honey, what we talked about? Always gotta work the mission."

Robin looked down, his face sad.

I gotta nip this in the bud. "Look at me," she said gently but firmly. Robin looked up. "You know I love you, but I got a job to do. The mission is what matters, right?"

This time, Robin didn't nod as quickly—but he did nod, and even gave her a little smile.

She smiled right back at him. "That's my boy. Come on." Grabbing Robin's left hand with her right one, she rose to her feet, and they started walking toward 72nd Street. They'd just take the CC uptown to Crowley's pad in the Ardsley building instead of downtown to the Gem.

Suddenly Robin slid his wet hand out of Nikki's, and he turned and ran back. Turning around, she called out, "Robin?"

He bent over and picked up Nikki's stake from the wet ground.

Chuckling, she said, "Thanks, baby boy. Now come on, let's get to Crowley's."

Been so focused on Darla, I didn't pay attention to what Crowley was saying about Spike. But I'm done with that—William the Bloody's gone on his last rampage, if I have anything to say about it. . . .

Chapter Ten

**New York City
July 10, 1977
12:10 a.m.**

Heathcliff cursed as they left the latest bar. They'd been all over the Village, dealing with the hippies and the beatniks and the other live bait that went into those joints. No sign of no British bloodsucker. The two of them had been going since sunset trying to find this dude, and now it was past midnight, and they hadn't found jack. Reet was not gonna be happy.

He looked over at his partner, who insisted on being called "Shades" on account of the large maroon plastic sunglasses he wore all the time. "Least it stopped rainin'. But if we don't find this cat soon, I'm gonna start rampagin'."

"I dig, brother, but if we don't find him—"

"I know, I know." Heathcliff thought a minute. "Look, he a punk honky, so why don't we go to that joint down on the Bowery?"

Shades gave him a look that would've been more effective if not for his eyewear. "Brother, can't you *read*? You saw the fuzz report on this dude—CBGB's was where he was last seen with those chicks he killed. He ain't gonna be goin' back there unless he a *total* fool."

"Maybe he *is* a total fool." Heathcliff sighed. "Look, we done tried everything else. What we got to lose, man? Worst comes to worst, we got a whole club full o' live bait to chew on."

For a minute, it looked like Shades was going to say something, but his mouth was hanging open for a couple of seconds before he said, "Yeah, okay. I'm fresh outta bright ideas. But let's take a cab."

Three empty cabs passed them by before one stopped to pick them up. Heathcliff wanted to eat the guy once they got to the Bowery, but Shades pointed out that it'd be stupid to kill one of the few cabbies who'd actually stop for two brothers. Heathcliff had to admit he had a point.

The sight they saw at CBGB's was enough to make Heathcliff want to vomit. *Dig them crazy threads.* There were dozens of white folks milling around and going in and out of the club with their spiky hair and ripped shirts and leather pants and metal studs and other crazy-ass fashions. One messed-up cat was wearing a shirt that was the British flag. Heathcliff tugged righteously on the wide lapels of his suit jacket and shook his Afro-covered head. "Let's wait over here," he said, pointing to the entrance to the Palace Hotel next to the joint.

"Say what?" Shades said. "We can't be—"

"He got to be comin' out eventually, man, and I *ain't* gonna be seen with those cats."

Shades started to say something, then looked at the crowd again. "Right on, man. Brothers got a rep to maintain, after all. These honkies belong in the NCAA."

Frowning, Heathcliff said, "Say what?"

"No Class At All."

Heathcliff laughed and took out a cigarette, offered it to Shades, then took one of his own. As he lit up, he asked, "You think the Yankees'll take the pennant this year?"

"Nah, man, it's the O's year. You seen Jim Palmer pitch? Who the Yankees got can match up to that?"

"You crazy." Heathcliff took a drag on his cigarette. "Yanks won the pennant last year, and this year they got the same team, 'cept they got Reggie Jackson now. Reggie can take anybody's ass over the fence, including Jim Palmer."

"Yanks got lucky last year, and then the Big Red Machine showed them what's what. 'Sides, Earl Weaver's forgot more 'bout managing than Billy Martin ever knew. Five bucks says the O's win the East."

Heathcliff laughed and shook his head. "I'll take your money, fool. The Yanks'll go all the way this year *and* next year and every year after *that*. They the best team in baseball."

"Fool, you livin' in the past. The Yanks ain't been nothin' since Mickey Mantle's day. Now *that* was a ballplayer. It's a damn shame he got hurt and let that good-for-nothing fool take the home run record back in sixty-one."

"They *both* fools," Heathcliff said. "'Sides, they ain't got the real home run record."

Shades threw up his hands. "Do *not* be talkin' 'bout Josh Gibson again."

"I *saw* Josh Gibson play, Shades. He made Babe Ruth look like Bucky Dent."

"Maybe, but he didn't play in no major leagues, so he don't count, you dig?"

Sighing, Heathcliff said, "Maybe, but I still say the Yankees'll win the pennant."

"No *way*. Hell, the *Mets*'ve been a better team than the damn Yankees."

Heathcliff snorted. "Not this year."

Barking a laugh, Shades said, "I heard that. Hirin' Joe Torre—what the hell *that* cat know about managin' a baseball team?"

They went on for a while, watching the crowd, especially when there was a pause between songs. The other reason Heathcliff wanted to stay outside was the music. Far as he was concerned, nobody'd made a single piece of music worth listening to since Leadbelly and Robert Johnson died, and this punk stuff was the worst. Just a bunch of angry white boys playing out of tune and screaming into microphones.

Thinking about Josh Gibson, who died just before Major League Baseball allowed black folks to play, Heathcliff thought, *Like they got a damn thing to be angry about.*

He was about to give up and try somewhere else when he caught a whiff of a vampire's scent. Looking around, he saw the spiky blond hair and the rest of the face that matched the description the fuzz had been given, down to the scar on his eyebrow.

Nudging Shades—who was in the middle of talking about his last meal, a hot little mama he picked up at Reet's club—Heathcliff said, "That's our man."

Shades took a final drag on his cigarette and then dropped it to the pavement. As he stepped on it, he shook his head. "What is that, a padlock on his neck? I do *not* get white folks."

Their target was standing outside the club, wearing a ripped black T-shirt and leather pants—plus the lock on a chain around his neck that Shades had noticed. Heathcliff had to admit that this one, unlike most of the people around him, pulled the look off. He looked like a fool, but a cool fool.

But still most definitely a fool, especially if he came back here. Heathcliff didn't see why anybody would come back to where they'd been eyeballed by folks that talked to the fuzz. That was just asking for trouble. They needed to get this punk to Reet's before he messed it up for everyone.

The vamp lit a cigarette of his own, then started walking the other way down the Bowery.

Heathcliff nodded to Shades. They split up,

Heathcliff going straight forward, while Shades worked his way up to the rooftops. They'd get the drop on him in a few minutes, once they got away from witnesses.

Staying at least twenty feet behind him, Heathcliff lit up another cigarette. The blond dude crossed Houston Street and then eventually turned left down Stanton Street. Heathcliff smiled. *Shades oughtta be able to take him there, and then we start rappin'.*

But when Heathcliff turned onto Stanton, there was no sign of his quarry.

What the hell—?

"Up here."

Heathcliff looked up to see the blond dude standing on a fire escape, his hand around Shades's neck and holding him over the side. Shades's specs had fallen off somewhere, and his brown eyes—which Heathcliff couldn't remember ever even seeing before—looked downright scared. His legs were dangling in the air over the street, like he was trying to ride a bike in the air.

How the hell'd he get the drop on Shades? Nobody *ever* got the drop on Shades, not even when he was alive, and certainly not in the fifty years since he got vamped.

"You've got twenty seconds to tell me why you're followin' me, mate—and make it good."

Heathcliff put his game face on and bared his fangs. "You ain't from around here, man, so maybe you don't know who you're messin' with."

The blond dude smiled. "Less a case of 'don't

know' as 'don't care.' Especially if it's you two amateurs. Ten seconds."

"Ain't me an' Shades I'm talkin' about, honky, it's Reet Weldon."

"And who's Reet Weldon when he's at home?"

"The baddest cat on the block, m'man. You mess with us, you mess with Reet, and don't *nobody* mess with Reet. You wanna suck blood in this town, you talk to Reet, you dig?"

"Sorry—not much for digging." He let go of Shades.

Shades, though, was a cool cat. He landed on his feet, put his hand to his throat, and glared up at the blond dude.

The blond guy smiled. "Look, mate, I'm not big on crowds these days. I also don't give a toss about your local politics. I'm just here to see the Ramones and have a little fun. So sod off, all right?"

Shades, his voice a little hoarse, said, "Don't *work* like that, fool! Now, you comin' with us to see Reet, or you goin' *down*, you got it?"

"Goin' down, eh? No problem."

With that, the punk leaped over the railing of the fire escape. Heathcliff ran to the side to keep from getting landed on.

The punk rolled on the ground and came up kicking—got Shades right in the stomach.

Heathcliff couldn't really follow what happened after that, even though he was in the fight. Both in life as a bouncer at the Cotton Club in the 1930s, and in unlife as a part of Reet's bloodsucker bruiser squad,

Heathcliff had been in plenty of rumbles, but he'd never seen anyone move the way this vamp did.

Now Heathcliff understood why this cat came back to CBGB's—it wasn't because he was too stupid not to return to the scene of the crime, it was that he didn't *care*. This was one *bad* mother. But that just made Heathcliff more determined. *We have* got *to get this cat on the payroll.* Not only would it make things better in the organization, but Reet would handsomely reward the vampires who brought this dude in to him.

The fight carried its way down Stanton and around the corner into Freeman, right up until the blond dude tossed Heathcliff into Shades. Heathcliff fell to the sidewalk, but Shades rolled and tumbled over to a pile of lumber that had been tied up in front of an apartment building.

Shades smiled, baring his fangs. He brought his fist down on one of the two-by-fours, smashing it to splinters, then picked two of the bigger splinters up. He tossed one to Heathcliff, who caught it with his left hand.

The vampire just laughed. "So you've got toys to play with now?"

"We warned you, man," Shades said.

"What, that you're a couple o' tossers? Worked that out on my own there, mate. This dance has been fun, but I'm gettin' bored. Can't believe the Slayer hasn't turned you two to mulch already."

Shades snarled and charged, the improvised stake raised over his head. The blond dude just stood there until the last second and dodged to his right, reaching up and grabbing Shades's wrist with his hand, then yanking it down and slamming the wood into Shades's chest.

A second later, Shades was dust.

Heathcliff couldn't believe it. He and Shades had been running together since before John F. Kennedy got shot. They were the team supreme, the dynamic duo, the cats who had it going *on*—where did this fool get off staking Shades?

Snarling and screaming to the night sky, Heathcliff ran right at his friend's killer, intending to do unto him what he did unto Shades.

The last thing he saw was the punk honky laughing; the last thing he felt was a hunk of wood slamming into his rib cage.

Spike dropped the sliver of two-by-four to the still-wet pavement and pulled out a cigarette. *Not a bad night*, he thought happily. *Tangled with the Slayer, saw the Ramones rock the joint, and killed two tossers. A fella could get used to this.*

Lighting the cigarette, he looked up at the rooftops. "Enjoy the show, pet?"

Nobody answered, but Spike didn't care. He knew the Slayer had been watching the entire fight, just as he knew that the two tossers who followed him so sloppily and fought him so poorly had no clue that she had been tailing all three of them. She was predictable, that one, but talented. Putting on his posh accent for the first time in a long time, Spike had put a call through to Nikki's Watcher's answering service and, all a-twitter, breathlessly informed this Crowley bloke that the Feast of Pohldak was tonight and that Sheep Meadow was the hot spot of choice. Sure enough, there was the Slayer in Sheep Meadow, ripe for the picking.

The fight that followed was a good one. Would've been Spike's last, too, if he hadn't done the recon—he was ready for the thrown stake.

Definitely gonna enjoy this one till I put her down.

He took a long drag on the cigarette, then headed back to the Bowery. The night was still young, and the fight had made him hungry.

Bernard was playing Connect Four with Robin when Nikki returned to the flat. The doorman called to let Bernard know she had come in, and one elevator ride later, she walked in the door.

The first thing she said upon entering was, "Why's he still up?"

Robin, who had just beaten Bernard and flipped open the hinged plastic bar that released the game pieces with a clatter, got up from the dining-room table and ran to hug Nikki's legs. "I'm sorry, Mama, I made Crowley let me stay up. I wanted to make sure you's okay."

"Under the circumstances . . . ," Bernard started.

Nikki nodded. "Yeah, okay." She got down on her knees. "But just this once, okay? It's *way* past your bedtime."

"I know," Robin said in a small voice. "I'm sorry."

"It's okay, baby boy, it's been a rough night." She pulled Robin into an embrace. "Let's get you to bed, okay?"

Bernard stood up. "I've already made up the guest room for him."

"Thanks." After shrugging out of her coat and tossing it onto the couch, Nikki took Robin's hand and walked with him to the hallway that led to the guest room (as well as Crowley's bedroom and the bathroom). That hallway was off the large space that served as both dining room and living room—the half near the small kitchen had the dining-room table where Bernard and Robin had been playing their game; the other half contained the sofa and two easy chairs. All available wall space in the entire room was covered in bookshelves that were full to bursting with tomes that ranged from the very ancient to the only slightly ancient—plus the occasional Dorothy L. Sayers novel thrown in for good measure.

While Nikki tucked Robin in, Bernard occupied himself by hanging her leather coat up on the rack, alongside his own coats and jackets that had lain dormant since March. He put on a kettle for tea, finished his cigarette, and began putting away the Connect Four game. The water was boiling by the time Nikki came back out.

"He was never going to sleep until he knew you were safe." Bernard switched off the burner, talking to Nikki through the shuttered window that allowed the kitchen's occupants to see the rest of the flat. "Thankfully, I had that game from the last time he stayed over, since I don't think he's quite ready for chess. Obviously your fight with William was a rough one."

Nikki sighed. "You got that right. He's goin' completely by Spike now, by the way—least according to him."

"Well, either way, you didn't stop long enough after dropping Robin off to tell me much about this Spike fellow, except that he was tough to kill." Bernard poured the boiling water over the leaves in the teapot.

"Tougher. I ain't tangled with a vamp this rough since Dracula." She fell more than sat on Bernard's couch. "Sorry for beating it so fast, but once it stopped raining, I wanted to try to track him down."

"Did you?"

She nodded. "I saw Heathcliff and Shades makin' the rounds, lookin' for Spike."

Bernard placed the teapot, two mugs, two spoons, a strainer, the sugar bowl, and a creamer onto a tray and brought it into the living room, placing it on the coffee table in front of the sofa next to the pile of books he'd been flipping through prior to Nikki and Robin's arrival. "On Reet's behalf, one presumes?"

"Yeah. Spike dusted 'em for their troubles."

That brought Bernard up short. "Really? Interesting— I would have thought Spike would want to ingratiate himself with the local vampire populace. That's his usual modus operandi—generally as a prelude to taking over said populace."

"Well, the only thing on that cat's mind right now is takin' me down. Maybe later he'll make a play for Reet's rackets, but for now? Nuh-uh."

Bernard placed the strainer on one of the mugs and started pouring. "Yes, but Reet isn't likely to give up just because two of his henchmen were killed."

"No way. And those two've been with Reet a *long* time. He ain't gonna take kindly to them bein' dusted." She leaned forward as Bernard moved the strainer to the other mug and poured. "We gotta be able to use that."

Before Bernard could ask what Nikki meant by that, the phone rang. "Excuse me," he said as he got up and walked over to the phone unit in the wall next to the kitchen. "Hallo?"

"Bernie, it's Arthur. I may have something for you." Detective Landesberg's phone call was apparently being made from a public pay phone, given the street noise that was clearly audible behind him. "At least, I hope it's something for you, 'cause I'm not sure this is something I *want* to handle."

"What is it, Detective?"

At that last word, Nikki looked up sharply. Bernard mouthed the words *calm down* at her, which just prompted her to snarl and continue fixing her tea.

Landesberg hesitated. "I'm down at Pier 88. A luxury liner just pulled in after a trip from England—except nobody disembarked. Harbormaster got a little cranky, so he sent someone on board to see what was what."

Again Landesberg hesitated, so Bernard prompted him. "And what did he find?"

"A whole lotta corpses. Some had their necks broken, some were stabbed in the heart, one was disemboweled, a few had slashed throats—and four of them, including the captain, were dead from exsanguination through bite marks in the carotid artery."

A vampire bite. "I'm assuming the constabulary isn't attributing *this* particular massacre to the Son of Sam?" Bernard asked dryly, by way of getting Landesberg to be more forthcoming.

"Nope. And we checked the passenger and crew manifest—everyone's accounted for except for one passenger. The name she gave is Anne Boleyn."

Bernard snorted at the obviously fake name. "So nice to see that the luxury liners are screening their passengers."

"Yeah. I checked out her cabin—it's full of dolls. I mean, *full*. My niece doesn't have that many dolls, and she cleans out Toys 'R' Us every Hannukah. Some nice ones, too—I'm kinda surprised she left them behind."

Damn. Damn, damn, damn. "I see."

"Look, Bernie, I know this is a bloodsucker. It's gotta be, I mean—nothing human would do this, right?"

"I should hope not."

"So any vamps you know fit this description?"

"One or two. Thank you, Detective, I'll be in touch."

Before Landesberg could say anything else, Bernard hung up the phone.

Nikki was stirring her tea. No doubt she had put in enough sugar to kill an army of diabetics, as usual. "You were talkin' to that detective, and you used the word 'massacre,' so I'm assumin' that wasn't good news."

"Hardly." He rejoined Nikki on the couch and took a sip of tea, in the vain hope that it might warm him— or at least comfort him. It did neither. "Based on Detective Landesberg's description of the carnage he has witnessed, not to mention the stateroom occupied by the likely perpetrator of said carnage, I would say it's very likely that Drusilla is in town."

"You sure?" Nikki asked.

Bernard nodded. "Unless there's another psychotic British female vampire with a fetish for dolls who'd have reason to come to New York, yes, I'm sure. She's Spike's sire, and the two have been inseparable for as long as anyone's been able to keep track of them—though, to be fair, we haven't been as successful at that as one would like. But from what accounts we do have, the pair of them are as devoted to each other as two demons can be." He picked up one of the books from the coffee table. "There's one particularly vivid description in the Watchers' archive from a decade and a half ago about a massacre at an orphanage in Vienna that the two of them perpetrated—killed two Watchers in the process, which, sad to say, is *why* we have such a vivid description." Bernard set the book back down and sighed. "The only thing that surprises me is that she left the dolls behind. I suspect the heat of the moment, or the fear of being discovered, caused that."

"She wasn't necessarily alone, neither," Nikki said in a tight voice.

Recognizing the source of that concern, Bernard quickly said, "Darla was not with her, of that you can be sure. We had two Watchers in Milan, and one of them reported that Darla's still there."

"One of them?"

Bitterly, Bernard said, "Yes, and he's sure because he witnessed Darla feeding on the other one."

Nikki winced. "I'm sorry, Crowley."

He waved it off. "That's all right—you've other things to be concerned with. Drusilla will try to find Spike, and she's likely to leave plenty of corpses in her wake. Add Reet's interest to the equation—"

"And we got us a bloodsucker bloodbath." Nikki took a sip of her tea and then smiled. "So if we're stuck with it anyhow, let's do it right."

Now Bernard frowned. "I beg your pardon?"

"Reet'll want revenge on Spike once he finds out what happened to Heathcliff and Shades."

"*If* he finds out."

Nikki's smile grew wider. "Any reason for me to keep it a secret?"

That got Bernard to smile as well. "I see your point."

Standing up, Nikki said, "Reet's boys found Spike pretty quick, they can probably find this Drusilla chick, too." She walked over to the coatrack. "'Specially if I tell 'em where to look." Putting on the coat, she said, "Looks like my night ain't done yet."

Also rising, Bernard said, "Good luck, Nikki."

Nodding, Nikki left the flat.

Bernard took another sip of tea, then set it down on the coffee table. He walked to the hallway, the hardwood floor creaking under his feet. The second bedroom had been converted into a study. Like the living room—and, if it came to that, the bedroom, the hallways, and even parts of the kitchen and bathroom—it was lined with bookcases, and it was here that Bernard kept his most important books. It also contained a daybed, and when he slowly opened the door, he saw Robin asleep in it. The boy was tossing and turning, and Bernard feared for the dreams he was having. Robin had witnessed his mother in action before, but it couldn't have been pleasant—especially with an unfamiliar bed in the equation.

But it couldn't be helped. Spike had somehow learned Nikki's name, and it was only a short journey from there to her place of residence. Bernard just hoped that Spike hadn't learned the name and/or location of Nikki's Watcher.

If he has, he'll find me a tougher opponent than most.

Closing the door, Bernard went back out to the living room. He loved being a Watcher, but he wished that the watching involved less waiting.

Be safe, Miss Wood, he thought as he lit another cigarette and poured himself some more tea.

Chapter Eleven

**New York City
July 10, 1977
1:30 a.m.**

About time my luck started changing, Charlie thought as he got the final hole card from the dealer—a young man with a large Afro, wearing a frilled tuxedo. He had given Charlie the nine of clubs, which matched up nicely with the other two hole cards he'd been dealt from the start—an ace and a jack of clubs—and the other two clubs he had in front of him. This gave him a flush, which was much more impressive than the three of a kind the other players probably figured he had, given the way he was betting. Not that it was totally off base for them to think—he actually did have three jacks. The way Charlie saw it, Lee had at least three kings—he couldn't have had a fourth one, because Clyde had one showing before he folded—and Pete was probably just bluffing.

This flush is guaranteed, he thought as Pete raised the bet by a hundred dollars, which Lee then raised *another* five hundred. Charlie calmly called; Pete stared at his cards for a while, then took a long drag on his cigarette and stroked the big feather that stuck out of the brim of his hat. Charlie kept his poker face on, but inside he was smiling—Pete only stroked the feather when he was bluffing.

Pete finally raised another five hundred. Lee studied his cards while puffing on his cigar, and then threw in another five hundred to call.

Confident in his ace-high flush, Charlie put in five hundred to also call. He didn't even hesitate, even though calling this bet would leave him with only fifty in chips. He leaned back and lit another cigarette of his own.

The dealer said, "Gentlemen, flip your cards."

Smiling broadly, his gold tooth showing, Charlie said, "You got the other king, don'tcha, my man?"

Lee nodded. "Yeah."

Charlie flipped over the ace, jack, and nine. "Well too bad, sucker, 'cause I got me an ace-high flush."

Giving Charlie a smile of his own, Lee calmly flipped over his other king—and the pair of fours he had to go with it. A full house, which beat a flush.

Son of a bitch! Charlie couldn't believe it. It was an ace-high flush! How could this fool beat him?

But beat him he did. Again. It was the fourth time

tonight Charlie had a sure-thing hand go bad on him.

The dealer used his rake to push all the chips in the center of the circular felt table toward Lee.

Disgusted, Charlie stubbed out his cigarette and got up from the table, grabbing his two twenty-five-dollar chips.

"Be cool, brother," Lee said. "It's just the way the game is played."

"Kiss my ass," Charlie muttered as he walked over to the blackjack table.

Shoulda known my luck would run out, Charlie thought. He'd been coming to this underground casino twice a month for the past year. Every other Saturday, like clockwork, Charlie would take the paycheck he'd gotten the previous day, cash it at the joint on Amsterdam Avenue, and then come here to make the money grow. Located in the basement of an apartment building on 125th Street, it was accessible only from an alley, and you had to pay fifty bucks just to get in the door.

But Charlie always made that fifty right back, with interest.

There was one time he didn't come because the place was closed. Apparently the dudes who ran the place got a tip-off that the cops would be raiding the joint, so they closed up shop till the heat blew over. Aside from that night, though, he was here the day after every payday.

Never until tonight, though, had he lost this badly.

Sure, he'd sometimes have a bad run—the cards wouldn't behave, or some sucker would get lucky—

but he always came back. He'd *never* been down to his last fifty dollars.

How'm I supposed to show Bernadette a good time if I ain't got no dough? Not to mention Vernetha—and I promised Claudette I'd take her to the movies after church on Sunday. What is a brother to do?

He sat dolefully at the blackjack table when some sister got up with a big pile of chips. The dealer—another big-afroed brother in a frilled tuxedo—dealt the cards, giving Charlie a jack and a king. He stood pat and put down all fifty on it—the other players either busted, or had less than twenty, and the dealer had a nine showing.

The dealer flipped his card and it showed an ace. He then took two cards from the deck—an ace and a ten.

Blackjack. Charlie had lost his last fifty on that bet.

Right when the dealer raked in the last of Charlie's chips, the door exploded with a deafening crack.

Throwing up his arms, Charlie ducked, then looked up to see a chick. She was wearing a long leather coat—in July, which was just nuts—and a big smile. "Game's over, suckers."

That door was the only way in or out that Charlie knew about. There was another door to some back room, but two large brothers guarded that door, and only dudes wearing those frilled tuxedos went back there.

Those two door guards, as well as the other guards, ran toward the chick. *That girl is dead meat.*

At the last possible second, the chick reared back

and kicked the guard in the face, knocking him to the floor.

Everything happened very quickly after that.

The chick spun around and kicked another guard with her other leg. Then the really freaky part happened: The guards' faces all changed somehow. Suddenly, instead of just being big scary mothers, they looked like something out of a Frankenstein movie or something. They started snarling and jumping at the chick.

She whipped something out of her coat—it looked like a big stick—and threw it at one of the guards. It nailed the guy right in the chest.

And then the guard just—just *exploded* into dust.

The whole place went nuts. People started screaming and running around, but the chick and the guards were all in the way of the only exit.

Charlie, though, was just staring at the pile of dust where the guard used to be. He couldn't breathe, his heart was pumping like a bass drum, and sweat was beading on his forehead. Some girl yelled at the top of her lungs, so loud that Charlie's ears hurt.

Two more guards jumped the chick, and Charlie figured she was done for, but somehow she managed to throw them off her—they landed right on the very poker table where Charlie had lost most of his money, smashing the thing to little pieces.

When the chick did a cartwheel, using it to kick another guard in the face, it got her away from the door.

Charlie saw his moment, but he couldn't get his

legs to move. Not that it mattered, since everyone else in the place was still screaming, but now they were all heading for the doorway with the busted door.

The chick grabbed a piece of the door and stabbed another guard with it.

He turned to dust too.

Suddenly, it all clicked. *The Slayer.* He'd been hearing stories about this chick for the past couple of years, but Charlie had always thought it was baloney—stuff kids told to scare the other kids, or that bums told while they were bored, or that people who watched too many stupid movies believed.

Now, though, Charlie believed. He had to beat it, and fast.

But his legs still wouldn't move.

One of the guards grabbed the Slayer and punched her hard enough to send her flying into the roulette table. She grabbed the roulette wheel, ripped it out of the table, and threw it like a Frisbee right at the guard's head.

It sliced the guard's head clean off, and then he turned to dust too.

"What you starin' at, fool?"

Charlie shook his head and looked at the Slayer, who'd said those words. With a start, he realized that he was the only person left in the casino who didn't work there, besides the Slayer.

She didn't have to tell him twice. He beat it out of there as fast as he could run.

I swear to God, he thought as he ran through the broken doorway and up the creaky wooden stairs to the safety of 125th Street, *I ain't never gonna gamble ever again. May the Lord strike me dead if I'm lying.*

He wondered if Bernadette was home. He for damn sure needed some comforting right now. . . .

After her unresolved fight with Spike, and after watching while he dusted two vamps, it was out of *sight* for Nikki to cut loose on some of Reet's bloodsuckers.

She recognized only one of them: Lucas, the dude who ran this gambling outfit. He was the one with the straight line to Reet, so he was the only one she didn't stake.

However, that didn't mean she couldn't knock him around a little.

Having already busted a poker table and a roulette wheel, she proceeded to knock vamps into the slot machines, both blackjack tables, and two other poker tables. By the time she dusted the last of the ones she intended to stake—and all the civilians had left, including that turkey who needed a kick in the ass to be convinced to beat it—the only item in the entire casino that was still in one piece was the fourth poker table.

She had known about this place for a while, thanks to Crowley—or, more accurately, thanks to his cop friend. But according to Landesberg, the fuzz couldn't bust the place. Every time they got a warrant and planned a raid, Reet got wind of it and cleared the joint. Given how many cops were in Reet's pocket, that didn't surprise Nikki at all.

Lucky for her, the Slayer didn't need a warrant.

Up until now, she hadn't bothered with the place because, of all of Reet's interests, this was the one that probably did the least harm. Nikki kept her focus on the drugs and prostitution ends of Reet's little bloodsucking empire. But she knew Lucas had been running this joint, and Lucas had Reet's ear. Tonight Nikki needed to put something in that ear.

Not that Lucas was gonna make it easy on her. He jumped at her and punched her right in the face. She almost didn't see it coming, what with the frilled-out white cuffs sticking out from under his tuxedo jacket—and even so, she was barely able to roll with it.

Stumbling back a step or two, she fell against the bar. Bracing herself on its edge, she did a double kick on Lucas's jaw. Then she reached behind the bar, grabbed a bottle, and broke it over Lucas's head.

Then she noticed that it was a bottle of Old Grand-Dad. "Damn—shouldn't be wastin' fine liquor on a sucker like you." Tossing the broken bottle to the floor, she grabbed the dazed Lucas, picked him up, and threw him down hard onto the last poker table, which shattered.

Lucas' Afro was all wet from the liquor and also full of splinters and bits of felt from the poker table. Nikki hauled him up to one of the chairs that was still upright and intact. After sticking him in the seat, she went behind the bar and found some dishrags. Grabbing three of them, she tied Lucas's wrists together behind the back of the chair, then tied each ankle to one of the chair legs.

Then she went back behind the bar and found a

bottle of rum. She'd reached drinking age two years ago, and while slaying meant not having too many chances to party, she had acquired a taste for rum. It certainly beat the hell out of that Scotch that Crowley liked, that was for *damn* sure. Stuff tasted like motor oil.

She'd gotten through only about an eighth of the bottle when Lucas finally woke up. "Wha—?" He looked around, struggled against his bonds, which made the chair inch forward on the thin-carpeted floor, then saw Nikki. "Aw, *man*. Whatchoo tyin' me up for, bitch?"

"We need to have a conversation, Lucas."

Lucas's big brown eyes got wider. "How you know my name?"

Nikki grinned and came out from behind the bar. "I know *all* about you, Lucas. And most of it? I don't give a damn. But I do know one thing—you talk to Reet."

"Girl, you think you gonna get to Reet through me, then you got another think comin', you dig?"

Shaking her head, Nikki said, "No, no, no, you don't get it, Lucas. See, I just want you to deliver a message."

Looking around the trashed casino, Lucas said, "What, this ain't it?"

"Nah, this was just my way o' gettin' your attention." She walked around to stand behind Lucas. She grabbed his nappy Afro, still damp with liquor, and pulled his head back so he was looking up at her. "See, we got us a mutual problem, me an' Reet. Name o' Spike."

Lucas looked confused. "Spike? What, that punk honky? Heathcliff and Shades are bringin' his white ass in."

"No, they ain't." Letting go of Lucas's head, Nikki walked around the chair so Lucas could face her head-on. Reaching into her pocket, she pulled out the item she'd retrieved from the fire escape of a downtown building after Spike grabbed Shades.

After she tossed the maroon plastic sunglasses to the floor, Lucas gasped and got his game face on. He struggled harder against his bonds, but the dishrags held. "Shades! You dusted Shades?"

"Nope. Spike did. They told him to come along to see Reet, and this was how Spike said no. He dusted 'em both."

"You're jivin' me, bitch! *You* killed 'em!"

"Now, why would I wanna lie about that, fool? What, you think I'm gonna get all shy about dustin' one o' you?"

Lucas frowned. "Yeah, that's true."

Nikki started pacing back and forth, kicking the debris of various tables around the room. "Believe me, if I dusted either one of those turkeys, I'd be gloatin'. But I ain't, 'cause I ain't done it. Spike did."

"He gonna *pay* for that."

"Shut up, fool, I'm talkin'!"

Lucas cringed.

Reaching down, Nikki picked up a poker chip and started flicking it between her fingers. "Y'see, Lucas, we got us a good thing goin' here. Reet does his business, I do my business—it's a system. It works. But Spike, he's jammin' up the works. And he's tough."

"He just some British honky! We'll beat his ass!"

Nikki leaned on the arms of the chair, putting her face right in Lucas's ugly one. "I *said* to shut up, fool. Spike dusted Heathcliff and Shades by himself. And I've gone two rounds with him. The sucker is *tough*." She stood up. Lucas had really bad breath. "But he got himself a weakness."

Lucas tried to lean forward in his chair, but couldn't. "What is it?"

"He got a honey. Another British chick, name o' Drusilla. She just blew into town." She looked right at Lucas. "You tell Reet—you find her, he can name his terms to Spike."

"That's it?" Lucas blinked. "Some bitch is supposed to—"

"Drusilla ain't just 'some bitch.' Spike's crazy about her. She's his sire. Also, she is stone-cold crazy. Got a thing for dolls, too, so maybe check out toy stores and department stores and stuff."

Shaking his head, Lucas said, "I don't get it—why you tellin' *me* this?"

"I ain't—I'm tellin' Reet through you. See, Spike's a problem for me, but he's a bigger problem for Reet. He killed two o' Reet's boys."

"Hell, girl, you killed six o' Reet's boys tonight!"

"How many times I gotta tell you to shut up, fool?" She pulled out her stake. "If you want, I'll dust your black ass right now and find someone else."

Lucas's gray, watery eyes grew wide. "Naw! Naw,

that's all right, mama, just put the stake down, okay?"

Still holding up the stake, Nikki said, "I'm the *Slayer*, baby—dustin' vamps is what I *do*. But Spike ain't no Slayer—he one o' you, and he be dustin' his own *kind*. That just ain't right."

"Right on, sister—look, I'll be tellin' Reet all this, I *promise*. Just put the stake down, okay?"

Grinning, Nikki lowered the stake. "Good." She moved toward the door, kicking aside playing cards, chips, bits of wood, and chairs. When she got to the door, she stopped, turned, and looked at Lucas. "Guess I trashed this place pretty good, huh?"

"You got *that* right," Lucas muttered. "Gonna take forever to fix this place back up."

"Yeah, but somethin's missin'." Nikki made as if to look around the room. Her eyes fell on the bar. "*Oh* yeah."

She walked purposefully toward the bar, kicking aside more gambling debris.

"Aw, no. No, baby, don't—"

Nikki vaulted over the bar and started smashing bottles. Alcohol of varying types spilled on her coat. Bottles of bourbon, Scotch, malt liquor, beer, vodka, rum, gin, and tons more all mixed in on the wooden shelves—which didn't stay intact for long.

After everything else that had been going on the last week, it felt good to just destroy something for no reason except that she felt like it.

"Bitch, you *crazy*! You know what it's gonna cost to replace all o' that? And that's assumin' that Reet don't go and stake my ass!"

Nikki went back to the door. "Just don't forget to tell Reet about Spike and Drusilla 'fore he does that."

With that, she left, whistling a happy tune.

Reet had known it was going to be a bad day from the moment he woke up in the evening.

As usual, he slept from before dawn till after dusk on Sunday in the basement of his building. He hadn't seen the sun for over a century, and he had no intention of getting acquainted with it any time soon. Besides, his business was such that most of the deals were done after dark. What little was accomplished in daylight was supervised by the few humans he kept on the payroll, plus a couple of demons who needed the cash and didn't have vampires' vulnerability to the sun.

However, as soon as he awakened, a good hour after sunset, one of those demons—a weaselly little Kulak demon named Ovrak—told him that the Slayer had trashed the casino on 125th Street Saturday night, killed all the vamps except Lucas, and tied him up.

Whatever other business there had been was postponed. Reet ordered his limo to take him to the casino.

Upon arrival, he saw several of his men cleaning up the joint, but the Slayer had done her work quite well. The booze for the bar could be replenished in a day or two, but it would take several weeks to order replacements for all the gambling equipment. *I only just finished paying off the damn slot machines.*

Leroy was already present. "I just called Atlantic

City about replacements, boss. And I got some other news too."

"That can wait." Reet looked around and saw Lucas helping to carry one of the shattered slot machines toward the front door—or, rather, front doorway, since the door itself was now kindling. "Lucas!"

"Oh!" Startled Lucas let his side of the slot machine drop to the floor.

The other vampire who'd been helping cursed at him for dropping his side, until he saw the reason for Lucas's utterance. "Sorry, Mr. Weldon. Yo, Tito! Help me out here!"

Leaving the others to continue removing the destroyed machinery, Reet walked with Leroy and Lucas over to the corner of the bar that was still in one piece.

"I'm sorry, Mr. Weldon, the Slayer, she—"

Holding up a hand, Reet said, "I know what the Slayer did, Lucas. I also know that she had a message for me. What is it?"

Reaching into a pocket, Lucas pulled out a pair of sunglasses that Reet recognized instantly.

"She killed Shades?"

"Shades *and* Heathcliff're dead, yeah," Lucas said, "but it ain't the Slayer that dusted 'em. It was that British dude they was after, Spike."

The name rang a small bell with Reet, but he couldn't place it—but then, he'd rarely bothered to familiarize himself with the vampiric community outside the tristate area. "He killed his own kind?"

"That's what she said."

"Ridiculous."

"Uh, boss?" Leroy said.

Reet turned to his lieutenant. "What?"

"Remember that other news I said I had? It was about this Spike cat. 'Fore you woke up, Andrés and I found that Spike turkey downtown, and he said—and I'm quotin' direct here—'Bugger off, or I'll dust you like I did those two tossers last night.'"

Shaking his head, Reet found himself boggled. True, he'd killed plenty of vampires in his time—most recently Mikey and his newly turned brother—but that was all part of business. All Heathcliff and Shades were tasked with doing was informing Spike of the way things were run in this town. *They were also two of my best. If this vampire killed them . . .*

Turning back to Lucas, Reet asked, "And the *Slayer* told you this? Why?"

"She said she knew how to get to Spike. He got a honey."

As Lucas told his boss about Drusilla, a memory nagged at Reet, and he finally realized where he'd heard the name Spike before. It was when that blond girl, Darla, came through town. Reet had been warned to stay away from her, as she was a favorite of the Master. Reet didn't have much truck with a vampire who called himself that—last man Reet called "master" died slowly by Reet's own hand on a Mississippi plantation over a century ago—but he also knew how powerful the head of the Order of Aurelius was. So he did as he was warned, but he for *damn* sure didn't like it.

That was the one and only time that Reet had been

grateful for the Slayer's presence in the Big Apple. The Chosen One had made his business into a nightmare, but at least she drove that blond bitch out of town.

After that, Reet had had his men check into Darla, and he now remembered that she used to run with a vampire couple named Spike and Drusilla. Reet never learned much beyond that, but it was enough.

"So Drusilla's in town too, eh?"

Nodding, Lucas said, "That's what the Slayer said. And she said if we nab her, we can get Spike."

"You believe this jive, boss?" Leroy asked.

"I do, in fact. Bonds among our kind are rare, but when they do exist, they are quite strong. Witness the friendship Heathcliff and Shades shared."

"Yeah, okay," Leroy said, "I can dig it—so where's that leave us?"

"We find this Drusilla girl. Take Andrés and Gustavo and track her down. Capture *only*—killing her will just enrage Spike. We want him to cooperate, and he'll only do that if he thinks we might spare her. If she dies, he will go after us, and that is not something we want."

Lucas said, "Slayer said she got a thing for dollies. Said to be checkin' toy stores and such."

"Okay." Leroy moved toward the phone behind the bar, which somehow had escaped the Slayer's wrath, and dialed a number. "What's happenin', Jonesy? Andrés still there? Good. Gustavo check in yet? Okay, when he does, tell him to meet me and Andrés at Macy's." He looked up at Reet. "We'll try there first, work our way uptown."

Reet nodded his approval. This Spike was a loose

cannon, and he had to be brought in line. No doubt that was why the Slayer had intervened. She had pecked away at Reet's organization. Profits had plummeted in the past four years, even though logic suggested that, what with the city's ongoing fiscal crisis, not to mention the huge rise in crime, unemployment, and inflation, his profits should have increased. The decline was attributable to the Slayer's efforts. Still, the girl understood how the system worked. She fought him the right way.

Spike, though, he was a wild card. For her as much as for Reet. They had a common goal—just as they had when Darla was in town. Reet stared down at the remains of one of the poker tables. The house couldn't always win if there were wild cards in the deck, because it made it much harder to predict the result. Reet didn't allow wild cards in his poker games—and he didn't allow them in his town.

Very soon now, Spike would be cast out of the deck.

Chapter Twelve

New York City
July 13, 1977
4:45 a.m.

"The sun's gonna be *up* soon, man!"

Leroy was gonna kill Gustavo if he didn't stop his complaining. "We got an hour, and the place is only up the street," he said as he drove his Cadillac down 57th Street. There wasn't hardly anyone on the street at this hour on Tuesday night—or, really, Wednesday morning—and FAO Schwarz was right ahead. They'd just come from Bloomingdale's and Alexander's, but no British vampire girl. Mind you, they'd seen signs of her. A bunch of dolls had been stolen from their kids' departments. Andrés had found a carbon copy of a theft report on one of the desks in the back offices of Bloomingdale's.

Then Andrés said that, since they were in the neighborhood, maybe they could check out Schwarz. It hadn't even occurred to Leroy—he didn't know nothin' about no kids' stores. But Andrés had been human more recently than the others, and he used to go there as a kid.

Each of the last two nights had turned up empty, and Leroy did *not* want to face Reet empty-handed when he woke up Wednesday night. If the bitch wasn't at Schwarz, he didn't know *what* he was gonna do.

He parked the Cadillac on 57th, right under a red sign that read NO STANDING ANY TIME. Leroy wasn't worried. If they got a ticket, Reet would fix it. If the car got towed, Reet would not only fix it, but give Leroy first shot at eating the turkey who done the deed.

Since Andrés was the one with breaking-and-entering skills, he went first. Reaching into the brim of his large purple hat, he pulled out some wires that he could pick locks with. He knelt down by the padlock that kept the metal grate over the back entrance to the store.

"This is *stupid*," Gustavo was saying. "This ain't gonna work. This fool gonna be here till the damn cows come home and the damn *sun* come up, and we gonna be crispy-fried!"

"Shut *up*, fool, I'm concentratin'," Andrés said.

Leroy, though, noticed something when he looked up in the window. "There's somebody in there!"

"What?" Gustavo looked up, then followed Leroy's gaze inside. "Prob'ly just a night watchman. We should beat it, 'fore—"

"Ain't no night watchman wearin' no dress." Leroy smiled as he caught sight of the long, frilly dress that trailed behind the figure moving about in the darkness. He couldn't make out a face, but that was *definitely* a chick.

He hit Andrés lightly on the arm. "Forget that, brother. If that chick got in, we can get in the way she went. She didn't trip no alarms."

Andrés didn't get up—he was still working on the lock. "We don't know that. They could have one o' them silent alarms."

"Then we gotta move fast. C'mon, let's check the front."

"Now you're talkin'," Gustavo muttered as Andrés reluctantly got to his feet.

The three of them walked down 56th Street to the front of the store—which was at the back end of a plaza that looked out onto Fifth Avenue. Leroy figured the place was probably crowded during the day, but at four forty-five in the morning, there wasn't anybody here.

What there was, though, was a smashed lock lying on the ground next to the revolving door that led inside.

"Ain't no way there's no alarm on this," Andrés said. "Or at least a guard or—"

He cut himself off. This time it was Leroy following his gaze: a night watchman, lying dead on the ground, puncture wounds in his neck.

"Great, so she's full," Gustavo said. "Let's get outta here before—"

"Will you *please* shut the hell up?" Leroy said. "Let's move, in case that night watchman has friends—or called the fuzz before he became breakfast." With that, he pushed his way through the revolving doors.

Andrés followed, then Gustavo. The latter was muttering to himself, but Leroy ignored him. They moved past the G.I. Joe toys and the stuff that was based on TV shows and movies and such, and went back into the area where the big stuffed animals were.

He heard her voice before he saw her. She was singing. "Three blind mice, three blind mice. See how they bite! See how they bite! They all chased after the princess, she bit them all in the neck, she did. Three blind mice."

"Very funny, bitch," Leroy said, "but that didn't rhyme."

The girl came out from behind a big display of teddy bears. She was clutching a porcelain doll in one hand and a small teddy bear in the other. Leroy was surprised to see that she was a *fine*-lookin' chick for a white girl, with big eyes and long, dark hair, and she was wearing a long white dress that was covered in lace.

"You just gotta be Drusilla," Leroy said.

She looked at him with those big eyes, tilting her head down so it was almost like she was looking at him through her eyelids. Leroy'd once had a girlfriend with a cat who looked like that. Or, at least, it did until Leroy strangled the cat and ate the girlfriend.

Drusilla started talking in a singsongy voice that

was hypnotic. "You're going to go all to pieces over a girl. The moonlight shines on her blond hair."

Yeah, like I'd be fallin' for a white chick. "You comin' with us, you dig? We work for—"

"The slave."

Now Leroy got nervous. "We be workin' for Reet Weldon. He ain't nobody's slave."

"Not anymore. He made the bad men pay. Now he wants to make me pay for another's badness. Shame, shame, naughty man!" Drusilla set the porcelain doll and the teddy bear down, and picked up something else—it was shaped like a soldier. "I found a nutcracker, like the one in the ballet. They were so delicious, the ballerinas. They tasted like daffodils."

This bitch is crazy, *with a capital* C. "That's great—but we gotta take you to Reet now, all right?" Leroy slowly moved forward. Andrés and Gustavo did likewise; the three of them started to close in on her.

"I don't think that's very nice. I think—"

"Hell with this," Gustavo said, and lunged for Drusilla.

She whirled around and slashed at him with her fingernails, ripping into his throat. Gustavo screamed and doubled over.

Andrés got his game face on and screamed, "Bitch!" He jumped at her so hard his hat fell off, and rolled it on the floor up against one of the teddy bear displays.

Drusilla broke off the lever on the back of the nutcracker and stabbed Andrés right in the heart.

Leroy was stunned—it all happened so fast, he barely had time to register it before Andrés was dust.

Now Drusilla had her game face on, but Leroy was stunned to realize that this made the bitch *less* scary. Like this, she was just another bloodsucker.

Gustavo kicked at her leg from his doubled-over position, which made her lose her footing. As she stumbled to the floor, Leroy grabbed her in a bear hug and picked her up off the floor. "That's enough outta you, bitch! Now you comin' with us to see Reet, and you try *anythin'*, you'll be dust, you dig?"

"Hell, dust the bitch *now*!" Gustavo said, clutching his throat with one hand. "She done *cut* me!"

Not wanting Drusilla to know that they were under orders to take her alive—since that would mess up any chance of threatening her—Leroy didn't say anything in answer to Gustavo. Instead, he squeezed Drusilla harder. "I said, you *dig*?"

"The salmon try to dig their own graves, but they must swim instead."

Rolling his eyes, Leroy said, "I'll take that as a yes." He turned to Gustavo. "Find somethin' to tie this bitch up with."

Looking royally pissed off, Gustavo asked, "Why I gotta be the one to—"

"Andrés had the fishing line."

Now Gustavo looked over at Andrés's hat, sitting on its side on the floor. Because it fell off before Drusilla stabbed him, it hadn't turned to dust like everything else on him—including the fishing line that was supposed to tie this bitch up.

"Yeah, okay." He walked off.

Drusilla didn't struggle at all once Leroy grabbed her. That didn't mean he was going to do something stupid like let go of her, though. But she was just talkin' garbage like she'd been all along.

"Darkness will come all round. It smothers like a blanket—suffocating everything in its wake and bringing the house down like a pile of cards. All the battles will come to an end, but one—and that will fester down the decades until it boils over like a stewpot."

Leroy muttered, "Right on, sister." *Where the hell is Gustavo? Only reason I ain't staked this bitch is because of Reet's say-so, but if I gotta listen to the chick that killed Andrés talk crap for much longer, I'll take the chance on pissing Reet off.*

Spike dropped his latest meal to the pavement of the alley behind the bar where he'd picked her up. He hadn't bothered with the whole take-her-home routine—too much work when he just wanted to nosh.

Wiping the bird's blood off his lips with the sleeve of his shirt, he wandered out into the humid Manhattan night.

Been four days since I tussled with the Slayer. Figure that gives her enough time to get right nervous, looking for Spike round every corner. Eventually, she'll finally figure I've given up or left town or some other such thing.

He sighed. The original plan had been to wait a week before striking, but Spike no longer fancied sticking around that long. *I'm bored. I've seen the Ramones, it's time to make a move on the Slayer.*

Before he got more than a block down whatever street this was—he looked up to see a yellow sign with black letters indicating that it was East 1st Street—he got a whiff of a vampire.

"I don't bloody be*lieve* this," he said as he stopped walking. "I thought I told you tossers to—"

"The name's Toby. Got a message for you from Reet Weldon, honky," the vampire said as he walked up to Spike. Toby was wearing tight pants that flared at the ankles—bell-bottoms, they were called, and right loony they looked too—and a button-down shirt that was completely unbuttoned, revealing a hairy dark chest. His hair extended at least a foot out from his scalp, held in slightly by a purple bandana he'd tied around his forehead.

"I don't care what your message is, mate. I didn't care when any of the other four tossers this Reet chap sent after me showed up either. I just want to hear some good music and bag me a Slayer. I should think you'd be grateful."

"You crazy? Grateful? I oughtta stake your ass for that—you killed Heathcliff and Shades, and Reet ain't gonna be *grateful* for that."

This is getting incredibly boring, Spike thought with a sigh. "Fine. Look, I'll take care of the Slayer, and then I'll be on my merry way, all right?" He started to walk forward, intending to move past the vampire.

However, Toby moved in front of Spike and put his hand on Spike's shoulder.

In a low, dangerous tone, Spike said, "Friendly word of advice, mate: I'd be moving that hand right quick."

Toby smiled. "You say you don't care what the message is—I say you *do* care, 'cause the message is that we got your honey."

Spike blinked. "My what?"

"Sweet chick, name o' Drusilla. We *got* her, sucker. Reet's keepin' her *on* ice for now, but she gonna go from *on* ice to *bein'* iced, you know what I'm sayin'?"

His mind reeled. *Drusilla's here? She came for me?* He smiled to himself. *She* did *come for me. That's my Dru!*

Then he realized what Toby was saying. *That bastard Weldon's got Dru.*

"You want her back, honky, you come up to Reet's place. Maybe we let her live. Maybe not. Better deal than you gave Heathcliff and Shades, dig?"

"I gave them a perfectly good deal—sod off or die. They chose not to sod off." Spike then grabbed Toby's wrist, which served to remove the vampire's hand from Spike's shoulder, and twisted it down, forcing Toby to his knees. "Now where exactly is Reet's place?"

Toby tried and failed to break free of Spike's grip. "Let—*go* o'—me—man!"

Pushing the arm down farther—and causing a snap of bone that sounded very much like a dried twig—Spike put on his game face and said, *"Where?"*

"Aaaaaahhh! He at that building on the corner o' Lenox an' 119th!"

"And which corner would that be?" Spike asked, pushing the broken bone a bit harder.

"Northeast! Northeast! You're killin' me!"

Spike let go. "No, mate. I ain't killin' you. I'd rather you suffered." For good measure, he kicked Toby in the ribs.

Then he walked over toward the next street. If he remembered right, there was a tube station nearby—or, rather, subway, as they called it over here. He had one hundred and eighteen blocks to traverse, if this Toby tosser was to be believed, and he didn't fancy doing it on foot.

I'm gonna get you, Dru. And then we'll kill every last one of them until we're swimming in their blood.

Just as he caught sight of a staircase that led to the subway, he found himself plunged into darkness.

It was an odd feeling. Spike, of course, hadn't felt the touch of sunlight in a hundred years, except for fleeting glances from comfortable shade. But a big city in the late twentieth century was never completely dark, even in the dead of night, and especially not New York City. Even in the early evening, like it was now, the place was brighter than Flanders Field on a sunny day.

Until now. None of the streetlights were lit, none of the buildings or advertisements glowed—only the headlamps from the cars still provided any kind of illumination.

A blackout, Spike realized after a moment, when he looked up Second Avenue to see that there were no lights, aside from car headlamps, to be seen at all. This city had, he knew, suffered a previous power outage a decade back or so, and now it looked like they had another one.

He started jogging north on Second. *On foot it is, then. Give the blood a chance to boil right and good before I take Dru back.*

"The storm gathers, but there is no lightning. Thunder, though, is aplenty. Why does the prince not see that his reign is to end in darkness?"

Reet Weldon stared at the vampire chick that Leroy had brought back. This was apparently Drusilla. Leroy had brought her in after Reet had already gone to bed, and he had some other business to take care of when he awakened Wednesday evening, so this was his first look at her. She didn't seem like much—but Reet probably didn't seem like much when Caleb turned him from a runaway slave into a creature of the night.

"She ever start making sense?" he asked Leroy.

His lieutenant snorted. "No way José. I'm tellin' you, boss, that bitch is nuttier than a fruitcake."

Walking over to the chair into which Leroy and Gustavo had bound her, Reet looked down at her. "You're the love of Spike's life, eh?"

Drusilla looked up at him with those big, brown eyes that made her look to Reet like a deranged deer. "I made Spike. He stopped being little Willy and became big Spike. And he'll come and burn down the house." She spoke strangely, the way British folks did, without pronouncing the first letter of "house." "You should have let him be. If you had, all your problems would be over."

Reet turned to Leroy. "Do you have the faintest notion what she's saying?"

Leroy threw up his hands. "Boss, I ain't followed a damn thing she said since we found her in the toy store. Like I said, nuttier than—"

"A fruitcake, yes." He turned back to her. "What Spike sees in you, I can't imagine."

Now she smiled at Reet, and it was the scariest smile Reet had seen in his long and eventful life as a vampire. "The same thing you all see—blood and death."

Just as Drusilla said the word "death," all the lights went out.

"What the hell—?"

"Who turned out the lights?"

"What's goin' on?"

Other shouts came from around Reet, but he ignored them. His first thought was: *Who's attacking us?* The obvious candidates were Spike or the Slayer. *But how could they have gotten to the fuse box? There's no way either one of them could have gotten past the guards without my knowing about it.*

Then Reet turned to the window and saw a sight he'd seen once before, on a brisk November day in 1965. The power had gone out all across the city. Outside, the only illumination came from the cars on the streets. All the streetlights, all the lights in the windows—which would normally be burning brightly in this mostly residential area—were out. The stores and churches and traffic lights had all gone dark.

"It's a blackout," he said, raising his voice over the din.

"Say what?"

"You kiddin' me?"

"Naw, man, he's right, look!"

Reet said, "You all know the drill!" Most of the vampires in his employ had been around twelve years earlier, and Reet had put measures into place to deal with a second blackout.

"Right on, boss," Leroy said. "Hobie, get down to the main entrance, check on the guards. Gustavo, whip out the flashlights and candles." There was a bump and a crash. "Watch y'damn step, fool! Curtis, take Georgie and—"

The phone on Reet's desk rang. Everyone was quiet for a second.

"Carry on, Leroy," Reet said as he slowly felt his way to the desk.

Leroy said, "Right on, boss."

Reet picked up the receiver. "Yes?"

"Mr. Weldon, it's—it's Toby."

Toby sounded like pure hell. Judging from the shouts and car horns behind him, he was calling from a pay phone. "What happened?"

"I don't know, Mr. Weldon, it's like someone turned the lights out all over or somethin'."

Sighing, Reet said, "I don't mean that—I know there's a blackout. I'm more concerned with Spike."

"He—he broke m'arm, Mr. Weldon! It's hurtin' somethin' serious, you know what I'm sayin'? Soon's I mentioned we had his girl, he went *crazy*. He's comin', Mr. Weldon—he's comin'."

"All right, Toby. Get back up here as fast as you can." The subways wouldn't be running, and Reet suspected cabs were about to become hot-ticket items. "Eat a cabbie if you have to, but get here."

"You got it, Mr. Weldon."

Reet hung up the phone. "Leroy!"

Cutting off his barking of orders, Leroy said, "What's happenin', boss?"

Suddenly a light shone in Reet's face. He held up a hand and waved it before it lowered toward the floor. When the spots cleared from his vision, Reet saw that Gustavo had come in with a flashlight and was now shining it on the floor. Casting about for Leroy's legs, he finally found them, clad as they were in purple pants and wing-tip shoes. "I want extra guards out front, as well as around our prisoner here. Spike, it seems, is on his way to claim his lady."

"Right on, boss."

That was when Drusilla started singing.

"Ring-a-ring-o' Rosies, pocket full of posies, ashes, ashes, all fall down."

Reet shuddered. *That is one crazy bitch.*

There is something fundamentally wrong with a world in which a university-educated Watcher is being beaten in Monopoly by a four-year-old.

That thought flashed through Bernard Crowley's mind as he rolled the two dice across the game board on his dining room table. He winced when he saw that the two numbers corresponded to the number of spaces between where his playing piece—the top hat—was and Park Place. Since Robin, who was playing the dog, owned Park Place and had already constructed four houses on it, Bernard was going to have to pay a steep rent. The price would enable the lad to build a hotel, driving the rent of Park Place up to its highest amount.

Grinning from ear to ear, Robin held out his right hand as Bernard placed the top hat onto the game space with the dark blue line on top. "Pay me, Crowley."

"You're quite the capitalist," Bernard muttered as he counted out the brightly colored game currency. It was one of several board games that had migrated from the Gem Theater to Bernard's Central Park West flat over the past few days. Bernard had been surprised to see Monopoly was one of them—he would have thought Robin would be too young for it—but the lad had proven to be distressingly proficient at the game. Given Robin's intelligence and curiosity, Bernard supposed it shouldn't have been *that* much of a shock.

Nikki hadn't seen hide nor hair of Spike since she'd observed his tussle with two of Reet's employees late Saturday night—nor, for that matter, had there been any sign of Drusilla since her rather dramatic entrance to these shores—but the Slayer was still justifiably concerned that he might come looking for her at the Gem. Nikki was, in fact, on her way there now to check in with young Mr. Manguson.

Since Bernard had become Robin's full-time guardian, he had finally given in and purchased an item he swore he'd never have in his house: a television set. Nikki had offered to simply bring up Robin's black-and-white, but Bernard had figured, in for a penny, in for a pound, and so he got a fourteen-inch color set, as well as a stand, which he placed in front of the bookcases between the two windows in the living room. (That was the spot in the flat that got the best reception. Since the stand was on wheels, Bernard could easily move it out of the way if he needed to access the books behind it.)

Having paid his rent on Park Place, Bernard sat back with his last fifty-two dollars and watched as Robin paid to have a hotel replace the four houses on Park Place—and, for good measure, added a third house to Boardwalk. Then the lad rolled the two dice.

"Go seven," Bernard said with a grin. If Robin rolled a seven, he'd land on Marvin Gardens, on which Bernard had built a hotel. A five or a four would do in a pinch, as he also owned Atlantic and Ventnor avenues, but they only had three houses each. None of those would be quite the windfall Robin had received from Bernard's visit to Park Place, but they wouldn't hurt.

Unfortunately, Robin rolled an eleven instead, putting him on Community Chest. The boy started giggling. He handed it to Bernard to read.

Bernard took one look at the card—which entitled the bearer to collect fifty dollars from each player—and handed all but his last two dollars to Robin. "At least I'll get my two hundred when I pass Go." He picked up the dice, hoping for a three, which would land him right on Go itself and entitle him to four hundred dollars rather than the usual two for simply passing it. That was a rule Bernard was unfamiliar with, but Robin insisted it was how Mama taught him to play.

Just at the moment, Bernard was grateful for that particular variation, particularly if the fates were kind and granted him a three.

Before he could complete the throw, however, the lights went out.

"Hell and damnation," Bernard said, "not the fuses again!" While this building had many charms, it was not of recent construction, and it had the wiring to prove it. Once Bernard had blown a fuse simply by making the mistake of running the toaster oven and an eggbeater off the same outlet.

"Crowley," said a little voice from a body Bernard could no longer see. "Look out the window."

Bernard did as Robin suggested—and felt his jaw drop open.

The living-room windows provided rather a nice view of the buildings to the south. On a clear night, Bernard could see the World Trade Center.

Now he couldn't see them, or much of anything else, without squinting. The lights had gone out all across the city. Even the perpetually illuminated tower of the Empire State Building was dark.

"Oh, dear."

"It's okay, Crowley," Robin said.

"How's that, Robin?" Bernard asked distractedly.

"Mama's out there. She'll take care of everything."

Bernard found himself warmed by a son's simple trust in his mother. Of course, Nikki certainly inspired that level of confidence, even in her Watcher.

But Bernard disliked the looks of the situation. There were any number of apocalyptic portents that began with the descent of darkness. While this could be a simple case of massive electrical failure, it could also be the beginning of something awful.

Under other circumstances, Bernard would light a few candles and start doing research, finding out what prophecy was about to try to come true.

But he had another responsibility right now, one that precluded too much talk of the end of the world.

I can do the first part, at least. Rising from the dining room table, Bernard said, "Come, Robin, let's fetch some candles." He mostly kept them around for rituals and the occasional spell, but they'd do quite nicely for illumination, especially since most of them were conveniently very large.

"Right on, Crowley—I gotta finish beatin' your butt."

Robin's smile was evident even without a decent light source. Bernard returned it, even though he was fairly sure the lad couldn't see it, then reached out for the boy's hand. He led him toward the kitchen, where he kept most of the candles.

As he and Robin prepared to hunker down for the night, Bernard cast a thought outward to his Slayer, Robin's mother, as she faced whatever it was that this darkness was prelude to.

Be safe, Miss Wood.

Chapter Thirteen

**New York City
July 13, 1977
8:30 p.m.**

A.J. was working the ticket booth when Nikki came by the Gem, which was showing *High Noon*. "What's happenin', Ayj?"

Shrugging, A.J. said, "Peg's sick. Marty's on his way in, but I gotta run the booth till then. You okay?"

"Yeah, I guess. Hey, there been—"

"No, Nik," A.J. said quickly, "there haven't been any British guys with blond hair asking about you—or about Robin. I've been keeping an eye out, and so've Leo, Alessio, Carmela, Marty, Harry, Wally, and Peg. Nobody's seen anything."

Nikki frowned. He'd just listed all the employees

of the Gem, but only Marty and A.J. knew what Nikki was. "What'd you tell—"

"I told everybody that some guy was hassling you and Robin and to let me or Marty know if he turned up. That's all."

She breathed a sigh of relief. "Thanks, sugar."

"Nothin' to it, Nik." He smiled. "That's what us landlords are for."

"Right on, Ayj." Nikki chuckled. "All right, I gotta get back uptown and then—"

Before she could continue, the entire street was plunged into darkness.

After a second, her eyes adjusted to the dusky dimness. The cars' headlights were still on, but the lights from all the movie theaters and sex shops, from the nearby skyscrapers, from the ads in Times Square—which kept the place lit brighter than day—had all gone out.

Twelve years ago, New York had suffered a citywide blackout. Nikki's parents were still alive then, and they'd told their eight-year-old daughter that there was nothing to be scared of, that they'd keep her safe from whatever monsters might come out in the dark.

Now Nikki's parents were dead, and she knew that there were real monsters that were several thousand times more scary than the imaginary phantoms of her childhood.

"Great," A.J. said. "I bet Mayor Beame forgot to give ConEd their kickbacks."

Nikki could only hope it was something that prosaic. She'd already stopped a few apocalypses in four years, and she knew that the universe had a bunch more up its sleeve—and some of them started with darkness.

Then she heard noises from inside the Gem, and she realized that the people inside the darkened theater might be panicking about now. She walked gingerly inside, not wanting to risk crashing into something. She could navigate the back stairs to her apartment and the projection room in the dark with little difficulty, but she hadn't moved around the rest of the theater all that much.

"What's going on?" said a heavily accented voice. That was Carmela, behind the concession stand.

"It's all right, Carmela, just a blackout."

"Nikki? Is that you?"

"Yeah, it's me. Just be cool, okay?"

"A.J. forgot to pay the electric bill, didn't he?"

"It's the whole city, Carmela." By this time Nikki had worked her way to the large double doors of the theater.

"*Dios mio.* Just what we need."

When Nikki opened the theater doors, a ton of voices were shouting at once. It was pitch-dark, and she wondered where Wally was. He was the usher on shift this evening, and he had a flashlight, but there was no sign of him.

"What's happening?"

"What's going on?"

"Oh, God, it's the Son of Sam!"

"We're gonna die!"

Nikki cried out over the din, "Everybody, *be cool!*

It's a blackout, just like the one in '65. Everything's gonna be okay, just come to the back here. It's all right, it's *not* the Son of Sam. Just come on back here and go home, all right? You'll be safe at home."

"I'm telling you, it's the Son of Sam!"

Before Nikki could again refute this, someone else said, "Shut up, bitch! Ain't no Son of Sam. Just the lights goin' out."

Wally finally showed up, his flashlight casting shadows on his long-haired, long-bearded face. "Sorry, man," he said. "I was, like, in the can."

Nikki said, "Everybody come back here—follow the flashlight, it'll be okay."

"We gonna get our money back?"

"Shut the hell up, Jimmy."

People started to file past Nikki, walking slowly at first, but the more people went through, the more lively their steps became.

One old woman asked as she walked by, "Do you work here?"

"No, ma'am, I—"

"Good—because if you did, you'd be out of uniform, and I'd report you to Mr. Manguson." With that, she exited.

A young woman, a sister, walked by Nikki and whispered, "You're the Slayer?"

Nikki just smiled.

The sister turned to her boyfriend and said, "I *told* you!"

Once everyone was out, Wally and A.J. checked the rest of the theater to make sure it was empty. Nikki took advantage of that lull in the action to grab the flashlight from Wally and run upstairs to her pad.

She breathed a sigh of relief when she shone the flashlight inside and saw that the place was untouched since she'd last been here on Monday to pick up some of Robin's things. She wouldn't have put it past Spike to break in without A.J. or anyone noticing and trash the place while looking for her.

Walking over to the tiny closet in Robin's bedroom, she pushed aside the old clothes and doodads of her parents and grandparents that she hadn't been able to part with but had nowhere else to put, and dug out the bag.

Crowley had gotten the bag from Poland a little while after he started training her—right when she first moved into the Gem, in fact. The Watcher had called it an emergency kit, and it included a bunch of weapons, some old pottery whose magical purpose Nikki had never learned, and a book and a box. Crowley hadn't said much about those last two beyond, "Pray we never need to use them."

For now, though, the main things she needed were the extra stakes. She had a feeling that a blackout was going to be feast night for the bloodsuckers.

After tucking the bag back into the closet, she went outside, just as Alessio was coming out of the projection room. He had a flashlight too. "Guess we're done, huh?"

"Looks like," Nikki said. "Let's get downstairs."

They slowly went down the creaky stairs to the lobby, where A.J., Wally, and Carmela were all standing.

A.J. said, "Ladies and gentlemen, the Gem Theater is closed for the night."

Wally shook his head. "Totally uncool, man. I guess we better beat it."

They all walked to the front of the theater. Nikki said, "I better get—"

Screams and the sound of shattered glass interrupted her.

"What was *that*?" Carmela asked.

"Dunno," A.J. said, "but I'm lockin' up the theater." He reached into the ticket booth and pulled out a long metal rod, then used it to hook a metal handle that stuck out of the top part of the Gem's entrance.

Nikki had never even noticed that before. "There's a grate for this place?"

A.J. nodded. "Uncle Olaf never uses it, since he's open all night, but I think now—" He tugged on it, but it didn't budge, so he tugged again, this time with two hands, but still to no avail. "Damn, it's stuck."

Shaking her head, Nikki said, "Let me, sugar." Taking the metal rod, she gave it a gentle pull with one hand.

With a loud rumble, the grate came falling down, hitting the sidewalk with a crash.

"Thanks, Nik," A.J. said with a grin.

Nikki heard more screams, and more glass breaking. *I do not like the sound of that.* Looking at the various employees, she said, "All of you stay together, okay? Which of you lives closest?"

"Ain't me, man," Wally said. "Brooklyn's, like, *far*, man, specially if there ain't no subways."

Carmela raised her hand. "I'm right over on Forty-seventh and Eleventh."

"Can you take in everyone for now? The subways won't be runnin', and I'm thinkin' buses and cabs'll be hard to come by."

"Okay," Carmela said. "I got lots of candles, too. We'll be fine. When I was growing up in Puerto Rico, we didn't have no electricity."

Alessio asked, "What about you, Nikki?"

Nikki hesitated, then said, for the benefit of those who didn't know she was the Chosen One, "I gotta find Robin. Be cool, y'all!"

With that, she ran down 42nd Street toward the noises. She passed by several porno theaters and peep-show houses, all of which had confused patrons milling around and angry owners closing up shop due to being powerless, just like the Gem had. Most of the women were scantily clad, and not just because of the hot weather, and most of the men were wearing trench coats, *despite* the hot weather.

Nikki had the feeling that things were going to get ugly. It was hot, it was humid, the city was going to hell (something that had literally almost happened six months earlier, but for Nikki's efforts), and now the power had gone out in the middle of the night. She did not think this was a good omen for peace and happiness.

Sure enough, when she turned the corner onto Eighth Avenue, there were a couple of kids breaking glass on the cars parked on the avenue. Chasing them off proved fairly simple—the sight of a woman in a big leather coat heading toward them had been enough to get them both to run away—but then she caught sight of two cars crashing into each other on 44th right at the mouth of the intersection.

Hell, the traffic lights are down. She ran north on Eighth, then ran faster when one of the cars—a Ford Pinto—started to catch fire. By the time she got to the intersection, the driver of the first car had gotten out and started screaming, while the Pinto remained on fire. There was a woman in the driver's seat, her body slumped across the steering wheel, and a young child crying in the passenger seat. The child, at least, had a seat belt on.

Tucking her hand inside the sleeve of her coat, Nikki grabbed the passenger-side door handle through the coat and pulled. It was locked, of course, so she pulled harder, breaking the lock. The heat from the fire—which, she now saw, had started on the floor in front of the child—hot on Nikki's face, she undid the seat belt and got the child out, ran to the corner, knelt down, and put her on the sidewalk. She looked over at the driver of the other car. "You! Get over here!"

"This ain't my fault!" the man said. "I was just drivin', this lady came outta—"

Getting up from her kneeling position, she ran to the driver and grabbed him by his T-shirt. "I *said* get over here, fool! Watch that child!"

The man was about to say something when Nikki forcibly yanked him over to the sidewalk. "Yeah, okay," he muttered.

Nikki then went back for the driver. She had a

large, bloody gash on her head and hadn't been wearing her seat belt. Nikki grabbed her, dragged her out of the car, then carried her over to the sidewalk next to the child. She looked around for a phone booth, then spotting one, said to the other driver, "Stay here."

Just as she ran to the phone booth, a vampire jumped in front of her. Grinning, the bloodsucker said, "Where were *you* when the lights went out?"

"Staking your sorry ass," Nikki said as she suited action to words. Moments later, she was at the phone booth, the dust of the vampire sticking to the soles of her platforms.

The bloodsuckers are gonna love this, she thought. She picked up the phone and dialed the operator.

She got a busy signal.

I don't believe this. How could the operator *have a busy signal?* After a second, she answered her own question. *Stuff like this is happening all over town.*

Then she heard the siren of a police car. Turning, she saw the car pulling up to the Pinto, which was now completely on fire and providing more illumination than anything else nearby. Two fuzz got out, one holding a fire extinguisher. *Good luck with that.* The other one went to check on the woman and the baby on the sidewalk.

Confident that the victims were in safe hands, she left the phone booth and continued running uptown. People were screaming and wondering what was happening. At the corner of 46th, some woman was proclaiming that Jesus was coming.

When she reached 47th, she saw a large vampire

attacking a young woman, and two more attacking two kids. To her horror, she realized that the two kids were the same ones she'd chased off from smashing car windows.

Pulling two stakes from her coat pocket, she threw one at the large vampire. As soon as he turned to dust, the woman he was attacking turned and ran like hell.

Meanwhile, she grabbed one of the other two just as he was about to bite the neck of one of the kids. She punched him in the face, which caused him to stagger backward, leaving him open to be staked.

As soon as he got dusted, his pal lost interest in his target, choosing instead to run away.

Nikki took the same stake she'd used on his partner and threw it at his back. A moment later he was dust too.

"Thanks, Slayer!" one of the kids said.

"You know who I am?" Nikki asked cautiously. Probably these kids just knew her rep, but she needed to be sure.

"Why you think we ran, mama?" the other one said with a grin. "Soon's we saw you, we figured you'd rough us up."

"Didn't think no vamps'd be trying to suck us dry, though," the first one said. "That was *not* cool."

Nikki shook her head. "Yeah, well, I catch you two bein' stupid again, and I *will* rough you up—and not nicely, like I did those bloodsuckers, you dig?"

"We dig, mama, we dig."

"Good. Now go on home." She looked around. "It ain't safe to be out tonight."

With that, she ran off in search of another phone booth. She needed to call Crowley, make sure Robin was okay....

It had taken Spike a couple of hours to make it all the way up to 119th Street. On the way, he'd been tempted by panic, chaos, disorder, and looting, but he ignored all of it. Under any other circumstances, he'd be reveling in it, of course. The craziness was right up there with the rioting in Peking back in 1900. Spike and Dru had done in their fair share of missionaries and revolutionaries—more the former, since pious people tasted better—before the Slayer showed up intending to stop them.

She'd failed.

Tasting the blood of a Slayer was the most amazing aphrodisiac Spike had ever encountered, and it was made all the more glorious by getting to immediately share it with Dru.

Now this Reet Weldon bastard had Dru. She'd traveled across an ocean to find him again, proving that she loved him more than anything in the world, and this bloody git was threatening her?

Not on your unlife, mate. You are mine.

Two of the buildings he passed on his way here were ablaze, as were several cars. Spike had to smile as he jogged to the corner of 119th and Lenox. *Times like this really bring out the best in humanity. This is the way it should be: chaos, destruction, death, fire. A real party, this.*

He fully intended to share in it with Dru once business was taken care of.

Two vampires were standing guard at the front entrance to the building. Spike grabbed the hood of a car that was parked across the street and proceeded to rip it off. The grinding sound of rended metal got the vamps' attention.

"You a *dead* man, sucker!" one of them said as he ran toward Spike, putting his game face on.

His compatriot did likewise, not saying anything.

Spike whipped his new toy around, using the sharp edge of the bent metal to slice through the vampires. One went straight through the neck, dusting him instantly. The other one, though, was taller, and Spike was only able to impale his left arm.

That was enough to make the vampire double over in agony, leaving Spike free to break his neck and rip his head off.

Two down.

Belatedly, Spike realized he should've left one alive to question. He needed to know where Dru was.

Sod it, I'll find her on my own. He ran in the front door, all traces of fatigue from the run of over a hundred blocks gone with the desire to find Drusilla.

He opened the door to see four vampires with guns standing at four spots on the staircase.

Bloody hell, he thought as he dove back out onto the stoop to avoid the flying bullets. They wouldn't kill him, but they still hurt quite a bit and would leave him helpless to get staked or beheaded or the like. Spike didn't do helpless, so he beat a hasty retreat.

All right—Plan B it is, then.

He ran down Lenox Avenue, in search of ammunition for Plan B—as soon as he figured out what that was....

Nikki's plan had been a simple one: Find vampires that were taking advantage of the blackout and stake them.

The reality turned out to be much different. In the two hours after the tussle on 47th and Eighth, she'd staked a dozen more vampires, but that was the least of what she saw.

There was looting everywhere.

Nikki remembered only bits and pieces of the last blackout, but she would never have described it as "ugly." It was just something that New Yorkers dealt with until it got fixed.

But New Yorkers had been dealing with a lot lately, and it looked like the blackout could be their breaking point. The city was starting to look like those news stories about Watts during the riots there. Cars were on fire or crashed into hydrants or telephone poles or other cars. Vampires were all over the place.

However, the thing she saw most was people breaking into stores, shattering windows, ripping into gratings, and taking whatever wasn't nailed down—and, in some cases, what was. Whatever couldn't be carried out was usually damaged beyond all repair.

At first Nikki didn't concern herself with all of that. She was the Slayer, and the mission was what mattered. The fuzz were there to keep a lid on this. Her job was to throw down with the bloodsuckers.

Except right now, the vampiric bloodsuckers were outnumbered by the human ones. Every store she saw—electronics places, furniture stores, delis, shoe stores, flower shops, stationery stores, drugstores, you name it—had people breaking in and stealing stuff. At one clothing store, she saw a young woman running out clutching a pile of jeans. "Seventeen ninety-nine for dungarees, my ass!" she shouted. "Ain't never payin' that now!"

Even then, she was able to keep her focus, especially when she saw a barber shop being invaded by four vamps who were feeding on the customers—at least they were, until Nikki dusted them.

"Thank God you're here," one of the customers—a sister with a *huge* Afro—said. "Now things gonna be put *right*."

One of the barbers, an older black man, said, "Girl, whatchoo talkin' 'bout?"

"That's the *Slayer*, fool," the sister said.

Eyes wide, the barber said, "You the Slayer for real? My *goodness*." He put his scissors down and put out his hands. "It's a pleasure to meet you. Shoulda known, what with that stake and all."

She returned the handshake with a smile, then asked, "You got a phone?"

"Yes ma'am, I most surely do." The barber reached behind a desk and pulled out a phone.

"Thank you," Nikki said as she picked it up and started dialing Crowley's number. She'd tried from five different phone booths as she worked her way through town but got a busy signal each time—and it was one of those fast busy signals you got when the lines were overwhelmed.

Unfortunately, after dialing the seven numbers to reach Crowley's place, she got the same signal. "Dammit."

The woman with the big Afro put her hand on Nikki's shoulder. "You got to be gettin' back out there, girl! It's *crazy*, and you the only one that can stop it."

Nikki hesitated. "I don't know that I—"

The barber said, "Hey now, stop pressuring the girl. She can't be doing *everything*."

Looking at the barber like she was crazy, the woman said, "Sure she can, fool—she's the *Slayer*. She the one who stopped the world comin' to an end during the bicentennial last summer!"

At that, Nikki couldn't help but smile. All she'd done on the Fourth of July last year—the two hundredth birthday of the United States, and a day of great celebrating all across the city—was keep a few demons from taking advantage of the festivities to make mischief. Nikki had seen what the end of the world might look like, and that definitely wasn't it.

"She'll stop the craziness. S'what she *does*!"

Quickly, Nikki said, "Gotta go—be careful, all right? It ain't safe out there."

"I heard *that*," the barber said, reaching into his pocket for a set of keys. Nikki hoped that meant that he was planning to lock the door behind her. Might not do much good, what with people breaking and entering all over town, but every little bit helped.

Then, farther up Ninth Avenue, she saw something that made her heart sink.

Armstrong and Son Furniture Emporium was a modest store on Ninth and 49th. It was owned by two Afro-Americans—Frank Armstrong and his son, Larry—who'd opened it about a decade before. They were among the first minorities to receive a loan from the Small Business Association in New York. Because of that, and because of their success, they were pillars of the community, a beacon to everyone who wanted to do better for themselves, who were beaten down by the despair and the poverty—at the very least, they saw that Frank and Larry made the dream work.

They hadn't abandoned the community, either. The store had sponsored a variety of after-school programs at several public schools and donated money to a drug treatment clinic at Roosevelt Hospital. Plus, they'd always employed kids from the neighborhood in the store and paid them better than minimum wage. Had there been one place that Nikki would have sworn up and down would be left alone tonight, it was Armstrong and Son.

Which made it that much more devastating to see half a dozen people rooting around through the store.

No vampires were present, no chaos demons trying to wreak havoc, no magic spell making all these people crazy. By that token, Nikki should've moved on, found a supernatural crisis she could sink her stake into and leave this to the fuzz.

"She'll stop the craziness. S'what she does!"

Grinding her teeth, Nikki dove through the broken

glass and shattered window guard of Armstrong and Son.

Over here, two people were carrying a sofa toward the door. Over there, someone was using a switchblade to slice open an easy chair. Three people were carrying an entire dining-room set out.

Nikki could only make out that much because of the flashlights shining down from the balcony level. Following the beams upward, Nikki was barely able to make out one of the two owners, probably Frank, yelling, "Stop that! Get outta here!"

Suddenly the dining-room carriers were doused with water. Cursing, they dropped the table and chairs and ran out. Nikki looked up to see Larry holding an upended bucket.

Neat trick, but that ain't gonna hold 'em off for long. Nikki had to do something. *But what? These people are human. I punch any one of them, I'll probably kill 'em.* From the very beginning, Crowley had drilled into her that she could not unleash her Slayer strength on regular humans, only vampires and demons. Robin, of all people, had reinforced it, taking the lessons of his favorite comic book heroes to heart. *Besides, a rumble will just make things worse for the Armstrongs.*

"What the hell's *wrong* with you people?" somebody shouted. To Nikki's shock, she realized that she herself was saying those words. She'd never been a talker—Crowley had taught her it was best to conserve her energy and not speak while fighting. Every once in a while, she'd speak up—to tell some fool to stop messing with her coat, or to make fun of them like she did Spike—but mostly she kept quiet, letting her fists and feet and stake do the talking.

Equally shocking was that everybody stopped moving for a second. Frank's flashlight shone down on her face, and Nikki refused to even blink. "This is Armstrong and Son. You know what this place *is*?"

"So what?" someone said.

"Yeah, man, it's time to get our own back."

Nikki couldn't see who was talking, but she didn't care much either, since she was talking to *all* of them. "Your own *what*? Yeah, life's pretty rough right now, but that ain't these people's fault. They been doin' everything they can to make things a little better—and you come in here and *wreck* their joint? That ain't payin' nobody back, that's just bein' a fool. You know what they say—we're lazy, we're no good, we should get jobs instead o' livin' on welfare, it's our fault for bein' in gangs, it's our fault for not takin' advantage. All you people are doin' right now is *provin' them right*. All you people are doin' is ruining the livelihood of a good man and his son, and for *what*? What you gonna prove here? All you doin' is pissin' where you live."

"Hey, man, ain't nobody standin' for nobody, so we got to *do* this!"

"Right on, brother! We on our own now."

"No," Nikki said, "you ain't. You got me. Some o' you may know who I am—I've been keepin' y'all safe for four years now, and I'll keep doin' it, long as I can. But I swear to each and every one of you that if you keep this up, I am *gone*—but not before I whup each of you upside the head, you dig? Now get *out* of here, and leave these people alone."

"Who the hell're *you*, bitch?" This was the dude with the switchblade.

"Shut up, man," someone else said in a whisper, "that's the *Slayer*."

"I ain't afraid of her." He walked up to her, waving the switchblade back and forth in what the fool probably thought was an intimidating style.

Then he slashed at Nikki's face. She ducked it without even trying hard, grabbed his wrist, and smashed it against her knee, causing him to lose his grip on the blade, then flipped him around and onto his back. Then she picked up the switchblade and snapped it in two.

"Anybody else wanna take a shot?"

Nobody said anything.

"Then beat it. Go home."

Slowly but surely, the would-be looters started trudging their way out of the store. She glowered at each one until they left.

By this time, Frank and Larry had come downstairs and were surveying the wreckage of their store with flashlights. Nikki caught only fleeting glimpses, but it didn't look pretty.

"Damn, mama, you couldn't o' got here an hour ago?" Larry asked. From what Nikki could see, he was a young man with a small Afro and a thin mustache.

"Shut up, boy—what'd I tell you about bein' fresh?" Frank snapped, then looked at Nikki with wide brown eyes that looked out from thick white eyebrows and a balding head. "I apologize for my son, miss."

"Yeah, I'm sorry," Larry said.

"That's all right," Nikki said, suddenly feeling uncomfortable. "I wish I coulda done more."

Larry snorted. "Doin' more than the fuzz."

Frank was shaking his head. "Look at this place. It wasn't much, but right now Armstrong and Son looks more like *Sanford and Son*."

"We got insurance," Larry said.

Nikki sighed. "Gonna be a lotta claims after tonight—there's lootin' *all* over."

Shining the flashlight back into Nikki's face, Frank said, "Then you'd best be goin', miss. We'll be all right."

"No." Nikki stood up straight. "I ain't lettin' nobody else take you two down. The community—"

"Is on fire. Look, I don't know who you really are, miss—I mean, I heard stories, but I never much believed 'em till tonight—but if you're as tough as I think you are, then the whole city needs you. We're just one store. We'll be all right."

"Soon's I'm gone," Nikki said, "those fools'll be back. Specially that turkey whose switchblade I broke. You got to let me—"

"If they come back, we'll deal with it. I couldn't live with myself if I knew that some other store got it worse—or somebody up and died—'cause we were monopolizing the Slayer."

"Damn, Dad, if she wants to stay—," Larry started.

"Shut *up*, boy," Frank said. "Go take inventory, see if anything's still in one piece."

Mumbling to himself, Larry wandered off.

Nikki said, "Mr. Armstrong, this whole night is bad news, and I—"

"Then get yourself out there, miss. Go where you're needed. Here was just the beginning."

Sighing, Nikki thought, *Actually, it's the middle.* "All right, Mr. Armstrong, if you're sure. Just one thing—you got a phone?"

Leroy Hawkins stood at the window of the third floor of Reet's building. He'd long since tuned out Drusilla. Next to him, Curtis was looking over at her, puffing on a cigarette. That cigarette was the only illumination in the room; Reet wanted to keep it dark in the room the prisoner was in, so no candles or flashlights.

"This is messed up," Leroy said, shaking his head.

"What is?" Curtis asked.

Pointing out the window, Leroy said, "This. We should be out there, man! The live bait is ripe for the *pickin'*. Instead, we sittin' in here babysittin' a crazy girl. It ain't *right*."

"It ain't right, but it is Reet, you dig, brother?"

Leroy shook his head. "Yeah, I dig." He looked back out the window. "You think that Spike honky'll come back?"

As Curtis pulled out another cigarette, Leroy said, "Hey, gimme one o' them."

Curtis took out his Zippo and a second cigarette. While he was lighting Leroy's, Drusilla started talking louder. "Fire brings light to the darkness. Fire opens the door. Fire takes it all down."

Curtis fixed Drusilla with a look, but Leroy just shrugged as he dragged on his cigarette. "Ain't nothing—s'what we get for lightin' up in front of her. Oughtta be takin' her to Bellevue, man."

Laughing, Curtis said, "Yeah, they got a bloodsucker ward down there?"

Leroy laughed with him. "Back at Schwarz, this bitch tells me I'm gonna go all to pieces over some blond chick. Can you *believe* that, man? I ain't never fallin' for no honky bitch."

"Maybe that ain't what she meant," Curtis said. "Maybe when she said all to pieces, she meant you'd be dusted by a blond chick."

"That is *whacked*, brother. Only chick who'd be icin' me is the Slayer, and she ain't no blond, you dig?" Then he caught something out of the corner of his eye. "Wuzzat?"

"What?" Curtis asked, and then joined him at the window.

At first Leroy didn't think it was anything—just another car on fire. With everything going down, that was the least of their problems. Long as it wasn't Leroy's Lincoln, it was cool.

Then he realized that something was wrong. "Curtis—is that car *movin'*?"

Curtis peered out the window. "What the *hell*—?"

With all the flames and stuff, Leroy wasn't sure what the make was, but the car was definitely on fire, and definitely moving down Lenox.

"That's some crazy—" Leroy cut himself off when the car turned—and started heading straight for the front door.

Before Leroy could say anything, the floor rocked, sending him crashing to the floor so hard he almost swallowed his cigarette.

"What the *hell* was that?" Curtis asked as he clambered to his feet.

Drusilla spoke before Leroy could: "The prince of darkness is come to rescue his queen and make love by the sunflowers."

That confirmed it for Leroy. "It's Spike."

"He was drivin' a car on fire? That's crazy!"

"Right on, brother," Leroy said. "Ain't a bitch in the world worth driving a burnin' car for."

The door opened, and Reet ran in. "The building's on fire! Some fool drove a car afire into the front door!" Looking at Drusilla, he added, "I assume it was your boyfriend."

"Don't worry, little slave," Drusilla said, "it will all be over soon. My Spike will come and take me to the promised land."

Reet backhanded her.

Tied to the chair as she was, the blow didn't knock Drusilla down, and when she looked back up, it was with that through-the-eyelids look that had scared Leroy back at Schwarz. "Nasty, nasty man. You want it rough, eh?"

It looked to Leroy like Reet was gonna backhand the bitch again, but he didn't. "Put her in the closet. I want to keep as many doors between her and Spike as possible."

"You got it, boss." Leroy went over to the closet to make sure that it had enough room for a crazy vampire. He shifted a couple of Reet's suits across the rack, pressing them against one another on the right-hand side of the closet. "All right—"

Suddenly, the door closed in his face. He heard a voice say, "Don't bother, mate. I'm here to take what's mine."

Getting down on one knee, Leroy peered through the keyhole. Spike was standing in the doorway, and Curtis and Reet were next to where Drusilla was tied up. Spike was all covered in burns and cuts, and grinning like a fool.

Reet said, "I'm not your 'mate,' Spike. And I suggest you—"

Spike was holding a piece of wood that had even more burn marks than Spike's face. "Your banister's all broken. What ain't on fire is in pieces like this." He reared his arm back and threw the piece of wood at Curtis.

Curtis was dust a second later. Leroy couldn't believe it; he'd made Curtis himself, at Reet's request, back in the late 1960s. He was a good bag man, tough, with good sense, and Reet figured it'd be best to keep him around longer than a few years and never let him get old. It had worked out pretty good—until now.

"That's a little trick I picked up from your Slayer," Spike was saying. "She's a tough bird, that one. I was all set to put her down when you had to go and gum up the works."

"There are *rules*," Reet said. "You broke them

when you killed Heathcliff and Shades and rejected my offer."

"Wasn't really much of an offer now, was it?" Spike was in the room now, having sauntered in. "More like a threat. I'm not much for threats—or for rules, when you get right down to it."

Leroy was starting to sweat—not so much from what he was seeing, but from some intense heat. Reet had said the building was on fire, and now it was spreading to where they were up on the third floor.

Spike was grinning now. "Your little empire's not much longer for this world, Weldon—the Visigoth's come over the bloody hill. Now you coulda just let it lie. I'd've killed the Slayer and been on the next boat home. You shoulda been grateful to me. Now, though, you've bollixed it up."

"You little punk, you think I'm afraid of you?" Reet didn't sound too good, despite what he was saying. *Why the hell ain't he attackin'?*

"Frankly, mate, I don't much care if you're afraid or not. I'll tell you this for free, though—your boys ain't comin'. Dusted 'em or dropped a banister on 'em or set 'em on fire. Only one left is you and a couple o' meat puppets that ought to be dying as soon as the fire spreads."

Then, *finally*, Reet jumped at Spike.

Leroy couldn't believe it—it was the lousiest lunge he'd ever seen. Spike just ducked out of the way and laughed at him as he fell to the floor.

"You been out of the killin' fields too long, Weldon. Lost your touch."

Reet got up, his game face on. Leroy realized to his surprise that he hadn't seen Reet go vamp for at least ten years, maybe longer. *I'm thinking that cat was right—Reet's been runnin' things so long, he ain't no good in a rumble.*

Spike kicked Reet in the head, then punched him in the stomach. Reet stumbled backward right into the closet door.

Leroy didn't move. Assuming Spike wasn't lying—and that sucker had no reason *to* lie—Reet and Leroy were the only bloodsuckers left alive in the building. Well, aside from Spike and his honey, but they didn't count.

Hell with this, boss—you on your own.

Meanwhile, Spike was untying Drusilla. He noticed the bruise on her face. "Did he hurt you, pet?" He sounded concerned. *Damn,* Leroy thought, *he really does love that crazy bitch.*

"Not as much as he wanted to," Drusilla said with a smile. "Or as much as I wanted to." She pouted. "Nasty man, wouldn't do as I asked or wanted."

Spike finished untying her, and she stood up, stretching her arms to the ceiling, then bringing them down around Spike's neck. "My prince come to rescue me."

"You came back for me, Dru—was the least I could do."

"I'm sorry I made you cross, my Spike. Do you forgive me?"

"Always, pet—always."

Leroy had to fight down nausea watching those two kiss.

Luckily, it was interrupted by Reet lunging at them. Spike broke off giving sugar to kick Reet in the face.

Yeah, I'm definitely *stayin' in the damn closet.*

Looking at Drusilla, Spike said, "Wanna do the honors, love?"

Drusilla got a look on her face like a little kid who'd been offered candy. "*May* I?"

"Of course, pet. You know I can deny you nothing."

She started clapping her hands together all rapid-fire-like, like the prissy bitch she was.

Reet, meanwhile, tried to get up again. "Can't . . . do . . . this . . . I'm—"

"You're *nothin'*, mate," Spike said with another kick to his face.

After he fell, Drusilla reached down and grabbed Reet's piece. It was an old .38 that Reet took off a cop he killed back in 1965. Leroy couldn't remember Reet ever firing the thing—for all he knew there weren't any bullets in it.

Drusilla fired it at Reet's left kneecap. As Reet screamed in agony, Leroy turned away from the keyhole, wincing. *Guess there* are *bullets.*

The crazy bitch shot Reet five more times, each shot in a different part of his body. Leroy looked back through the keyhole to see Drusilla kneeling down at Reet's prone form.

"Soon you'll be a slave no more."

Reet spit blood in her face. "Ain't . . . no . . . slave . . . bitch."

Drusilla grabbed his ears and smiled. "We're *all* slaves to our nature, it's just a question of accepting the bondage. But now, my little slave—you're free."

With that, she ripped Reet's head off.

Leroy fought harder to keep the bile down as Reet turned to dust. *That bitch is bad news. Never shoulda took her in the first place. Shoulda listened to Gustavo, man. Damn.*

The heat in the closet grew worse. Leroy could now see flames licking into the room.

"Time to bugger off, love," Spike said. "I'd say this calls for a celebration, don't you think?"

"We'll paint the town red," Drusilla said with a smile.

"Damn right."

And off they went, arm in arm.

Leroy counted to twenty, then opened the closet door and ran like hell through the inferno that Reet's building had become. Eventually, he made it to the street. All the way down, he heard screams and wails, and he saw Marv's and Gene's bodies lying on the burning floor.

Without even looking back, he headed to the gambling joint on 125th. It was still closed up on account of the new equipment from Atlantic City being late, but it was a place Leroy could hole up while he figured out his next move.

Reet's dead. So're Curtis and half the rest of his dudes. Time for Leroy to be steppin' up.

Chapter Fourteen

**New York City
July 14, 1977
5:45 a.m.**

As the sun came up, Nikki Wood stood at the corner of 119th and Lenox, mouth agape.

It's gone.

Remnants of the superstructure of Reet's building were still intact, of course, but most of the building was ashes and debris. There were also the burned-out remains of a car in the middle of it.

It was hardly the first building that had burned to the ground—or the first car set afire—on the night of New York's second big blackout, but the last one Nikki would've expected.

She'd spent the entire night fighting to keep order

in an increasingly chaotic situation. The events that played out in Armstrong and Son had repeated themselves all over the city, and rarely was she as successful in defusing the situation as she had been there, though she had been able to prevent at least some looting.

And she had staked more than three dozen vampires. In a way, the blackout had done her a favor: By bringing the bloodsuckers out in full force, it gave her a chance to put the biggest dent in the local vamp population she'd managed in any single night in four years.

Since she had been working her way northward, it was inevitable that she'd wind up at Reet's building.

Suddenly one of the charred, broken support beams that had crashed flat onto the debris started to move.

A vampire came out and caught fire as soon as he was touched by sunlight. Cursing, he put the beam back over his head, but still screamed in pain.

Nikki ran over and recognized Gustavo, one of Reet's boys. It took her a second to realize it was him, as he was covered in burns and cuts and bruises. "Not lookin' so good there, Gustavo."

"Slayer," Gustavo said weakly. "Well, don't this beat all. Bad enough we get the business from one of our own, now you gotta show up."

"What do you mean?" Nikki asked, though she had a good idea of the answer.

"That British honky. He came to rescue his girl—burned the whole damn place down. Killed Curtis and Hobie and Georgie and Lucas and Toby—mighta got

Leroy, too, I didn't see—and then ripped Reet's head right off. Then they both waltzed outta here just 'fore the damn building came down. And now I think my damn leg's broken, and it's daylight."

Nikki broke into a huge grin. *It worked! After three days, I was starting to think Reet's boys would mess it up, but they did it! They got Drusilla, and Spike got them.* Part of her had been hoping that Reet would take care of Spike and Drusilla instead of the other way around—like Crowley'd said more than once, better the devil you know—but mostly Nikki was just glad that one of her big problems had been kind enough to take care of her other one. *And all it took was trashing one casino. Outta sight!*

"Gustavo, my man," she said, grabbing the support beam, "you have made my *day*. You know what your reward is?"

Looking at her suspiciously, Gustavo asked, "What?"

She lifted the beam. Gustavo caught fire again, this time being consumed by the flames and transforming to lifeless dust.

"Same reward you'd get anyhow, sucker."

She got to her feet, the hot wind whipping her leather coat behind her as she walked down Lenox Avenue. A phone booth across the street caught her eye. She'd been trying all night, but she had yet to get through to Crowley. At least the busy signal meant she hadn't actually lost any dimes—except to that one phone booth on 98th Street that ate the coin—but she was worried about her baby boy.

This time, after dialing Crowley's number, she got

an actual ring. "Hallo," Crowley's groggy voice said after the third ring.

"Crowley, it's me."

No longer remotely groggy, Crowley said, "Nikki! You're all right! What happened?"

"I'll tell you the whole story when I get back to you, I promise, but first, I gotta talk to Robin."

"He's asleep—hold on, I'll get him." A clunking noise signaled that he'd put the phone down. Nikki bounced back and forth on the balls of her feet, suddenly full of nervous energy, hitting against the glass door of the phone booth as she rocked back.

Then, finally, her son's voice said, "'Lo?"

"It's me, baby boy. You okay?"

"Mama? Is that you?"

"You bet, Robin."

"Outta sight! I told Crowley you'd be okay!"

Nikki laughed, tears running down her cheek. "I bet you did, Robin. I had a long night, and I'm comin' back to you, okay?"

"Did you take care of the bad guys?"

"Yup." She looked over at the ruin of Reet's building. "More than I expected to."

"Outta sight and dy-no-mite!"

Again, Nikki laughed. "Put Crowley back on, okay, Robin honey? I love you."

"I love you, too, Mama."

A second later Crowley said, "I'm glad you're safe, Nikki."

"I'm better than safe, Crowley—it worked. Reet's people found Drusilla, and Spike found Reet. I'm standing across the street from Reet's burned-down building right now. Reet's dead, and so're most of his boys."

"So your plan worked?"

Frowning, Nikki said, "You thought it wouldn't? What kinda Watcher are you, anyhow, not trustin' your Slayer?"

"Well, I'm simply recalling your brilliant plan against those Pumbo demons. Took *months* to get the smell out of the carpet."

"Yeah, well, if you'd *told* me that they were allergic to leather . . ."

Crowley laughed. "All right, all right. However, there's a more legitimate concern. With Reet gone, rival gangs will be jockeying for position. Or perhaps the Mafia will move in." He pronounced it with a short *a* on the first syllable, the way British people did.

"That ain't my problem," Nikki said, "'less they're bloodsuckers. Anyhow, we'll cross that bridge when we get to it, Crowley, you dig?"

"I do indeed." A pause. "It's good to hear your voice, Nikki. I was worried. One of the neighbors has a transistor radio, so we were able to hear some news reports. It sounded rather ugly out there."

"It was worse than it sounded, believe me. But I did what I could. You heard anything about when the power'll be back on?"

"I'm afraid not."

"All right. I'm gonna head back down to you."

"Excellent. I'll have a pot of tea on."

Usually Nikki drank Crowley's tea only to be

polite, but this morning, she for damn sure needed it. And his gas stove would still be working. "Lookin' forward to it. See you soon."

She hung up and opened the door to the phone booth, the humid air blasting her in the face.

Maybe she'd be able to find a bus to take her back to Times Square. No way she'd find a cab in Harlem this time of morning—or any time, if it came right down to it—but she was exhausted and didn't really want to walk.

Still and all, she'd done some good tonight. *And Reet's dead. I ain't gonna complain about that.*

Chapter Fifteen

**New York City
July 14, 1977
11:40 p.m.**

The neon lights of the city were dimmed in Central Park as Spike and Drusilla rode a horse-drawn carriage up one of the transverses.

Power had at last been restored to the city twenty-five hours after it had gone out. Spike had to admit, after running through half of Manhattan in near total darkness, that he liked it better when the city glowed.

Certainly, he himself was glowing—he had Drusilla back. "I missed you," he said as he whipped the horse with the reins.

Next to him up front, Drusilla smiled that mischievous smile of hers and said, "My love will simply have to improve his aim, then."

Laughing, Spike gave her a quick peck on the lips. Were he not trying to control the horses, he'd have given her more, but he had to keep an eye on the beasts.

Normally, of course, the driver would be the one steering, but he was far too busy being dead in the carriage. For some reason, he'd refused to accept Spike and Dru's patronage because he wanted to go off shift.

So Spike and Dru took him off shift permanently.

They had spent the entire night making love amongst the daffodils in the park's flower garden, then found shelter during the sunlight hours. After sunset, they had gone to a local pub to have a drink and a bite to eat—the beer was wretched, thanks to the lack of refrigeration, but the bartender was quite tasty—and Dru had suggested the carriage ride. They grabbed one on Central Park South, and away they went.

As they turned a corner, a voice said, "You know, I should thank you two."

Recognizing the voice from this very park a few nights back, Spike pulled hard on the reins, bringing the horse to a stop.

A very attractive young woman wearing the most fetching leather coat Spike had ever seen leaped down from a tree branch onto the pavement in front of the horse just as the beast came to a complete halt, making a snorting noise as it did so.

"Well, well, well," Spike said, "if it isn't Nikki the Vampire Slayer. Thank me for what, exactly?"

She was shaking her head, as if in amazement at something. "It was like droppin' a dime in the jukebox and just waitin' for the song to come around."

Spike frowned. "What're you on about, Slayer?"

"The puppeteer yanks the strings, and we all begin to dance once again," Drusilla said with a smile.

Ignoring Dru, Nikki said, "Reet. I figured if I told them about your sweetie pie here, they'd nab her, and you'd go after them. Either Reet would turn your ass to dust, in which case I got one problem off my back—or you'd take care o' Reet."

For a second, Spike just stared blankly at the pretty face that stood before him.

Then he put it all together: how Reet knew about Drusilla being in town, how he knew about her relationship with Spike. *Her Watcher's probably got a diary or something that talks all about us.*

He threw his head back and laughed. "Oh, you are a ballsy one, you. Got yourself two enemies, so you set us against each other. Nice!"

"That was the plan. Once I dust you two, I can retire."

Grinning, Spike put his game face on. "Well, we'll just have to see about that, won't we, love?"

"I told you before," she said, taking out a stake, "I ain't your love." She threw it right at Drusilla.

Spike was able to lean over and deflect the stake before it could hit his sire's heart, but the Slayer took advantage of that to do a somersault, pivoting on the back of the horse, and kick Spike in the small of his back, which was left exposed when he deflected the stake. Wincing with the sharp pain, Spike fell to the pavement.

He looked up to see Drusilla going at it with the Slayer. Dru was a magnificent woman, but she wasn't much in a scrap—especially not against this Slayer's brutality. Clambering to his feet, Spike leaped and tackled Nikki, sending them both careening off the other side of the carriage.

That was enough to spook the horse. The bloody animal started galloping.

Sadly, Spike was in no position to try to rein the thing in, as he was getting his face punched.

He managed to block one of the Slayer's blows, then get a kick in, but it barely slowed her down. They rolled around on the pavement, neither of them getting the upper hand for more than a second—though in Spike's case, that was due in part to his keeping an eye on the trajectory of the carriage.

Once it went out of sight, Spike went a bit more on the offensive, throwing punches and kicks to beat the band, matching the Slayer's brutality move for move.

Somehow, he managed to get a kick to her head that sent her sprawling toward the very tree she'd been hiding in.

Then, much as it galled him to do it, he ran.

She's a cunning one, she is, he thought as he went after the carriage. *Played me like a two-bob fiddle and got me to solve her vampire problem for her. And she tracked us to the park. Some smarts on that one.* The Chinese Slayer, Spike had sought her out, eventually finding her in the midst of the chaos of the Boxer

Rebellion. But when faced with similar chaos in New York, Spike instead danced to Nikki's tune.

Turning round a bend, Spike saw the carriage picking up speed and heading toward the park exit at Columbus Circle.

I'm never going to get to it before it hits the street. It was late enough at night that there weren't many people about in the park itself—it wasn't safe after dark, after all—but once the carriage got outside the walls of Central Park, Drusilla would be in serious danger.

Pumping his legs faster, Spike ran toward the carriage, hoping he'd beat it to the street. Not that he cared if a few meat puppets got trampled, but he had gone to all the trouble of starting a massacre to get Dru back in his arms, and wasn't about to lose her now because a horse couldn't hold it together.

Just as the carriage went out onto the sidewalk on which sat the statue of Christopher Columbus, Spike jumped up, landed on the back wheel with one foot, and pushed off it to launch himself onto the top.

Drusilla was unconscious in the driver's seat, but Spike managed to move her gently to the side while he grabbed for the reins. Pulling as hard as he could, he got the horse to stop—

—right in the middle of the street.

Grabbing Dru, he managed to jump off the carriage right before a bus slammed into it. Suddenly freed of its bondage, the horse galloped off toward the New York Coliseum.

As Spike gently set Dru down on one of the

benches alongside the wall that separated the sidewalk from the park, the Slayer came running out of the exit. Barely pausing to switch strides, she gave Spike a roundhouse kick to the face, knocking him down to the dirty pavement. He managed to get in a quick kick to her stomach from the ground, but the only thing he actually kicked was her coat. *Damn, that thing isn't just pretty, it's practical. Makes it hard to judge where she really is.*

But the Slayer made her first mistake when she broke off fighting Spike to go for Dru. Spike clambered to his feet and leaped onto Nikki's back, trying the same trick he had in the park, and he wasn't letting a garbage can distract him *this* time.

Baring his fangs, he went for the Slayer's neck. . . .

You ain't getting me that way twice, honky, Nikki thought as she brought her thick platform heels down on Spike's booted feet in rapid succession, then—just as she had the last time he grabbed her from behind—head-butted him, and finally elbowed him with each elbow. It sent him stumbling backward toward the street.

Was hoping to do the easy kill with Drusilla, but I guess I ain't that lucky. Not that she objected to beating Spike first—in fact, she was probably better off. If Spike was really that devoted to her—and he torched Reet's place just to get her back, so he probably was—then dusting his best girl might just get him riled.

Spike was grinning at her as she turned around to face him. He was wearing dungarees with holes in them and a black T-shirt, like last time, but no leather jacket—unsurprising, given the heat and humidity, even this late at night. This shirt was different, though—it was a muscle shirt, with a tear down the top of the chest, and it was covered with safety pins.

"You are a tough one, pet."

Nikki decided she liked "love" better. "I ain't your pet, neither," she said as she lunged forward with a punch, which he deflected, then another, which he didn't.

Definitely better to save Drusilla for when I'm done. Right now, Spike was having fun. He'd been talking all sorts of jive in the park the other day about dancing and music—this was just a game to him, and he was having fun. If his sweetheart got dusted, he might start taking this more seriously, and Nikki didn't want him that focused.

Their tussle took them into the street. This late at night, there wasn't as much vehicular traffic, but they were drawing a crowd. Across from the park's exit, a bunch of people were walking in various directions, departing whatever event had been going on at the Coliseum that night. Here by the statue, a few others were watching the fight with horror or glee.

"Man, somebody should call the fuzz."

"Right on, brother—*you* call 'em."

"Kick whitey's ass, soul sister!"

"Show that bitch what's what, my man!"

I love this town, she thought wryly as she got in a kick to Spike's torso, then another to his chin. Before he had a chance to recover, she lunged with a right haymaker to his temple—

—which he grabbed before it could strike. Not missing a beat, she kicked him in the groin, which got him to let go of her right fist while she used her left to sock him in the jaw.

She kept at him, punching and kicking and punching and kicking. The fight had now taken them all the way over to where Central Park West and Broadway joined up, right by a subway entrance.

As she prepared to put him down, right here at the top of the stairs, he surprised her with a gut punch, knocking the wind right out of her. Doubled over, she fell to her knees for a second, hoping to lull him into thinking she was worse off than she was.

When he moved in for the kill, she rolled onto her back and kicked out with both feet. Only one foot actually got Spike, but it knocked him straight back and down the wide staircase to the subway.

Dammit, didn't mean to do that. She got to her feet and ran down the stairs after him, but he had gotten up from the bottom of the stairs and kept running *into* the station. *What the hell's he doin'?*

Then she figured it out. *He's protecting Drusilla by getting me away from her. No problem—I can always come back for her.*

An old white guy sat in the token booth and looked completely uninterested in the fact that someone had just jumped his fare. Spike had leaped over the large wooden turnstile and then headed straight for the IND track downstairs instead of the IRT track that was right there.

Nikki leaped over the turnstile herself—*if the clerk*

don't care about Spike, he ain't gonna care about me, and I got little enough bread as it is without spending fifty cents just to chase a bloodsucker—and ran after Spike, figuring that he wanted to be down below with the rest of the rats.

As she ran down after him, she heard the PA system go off, but it was the usual incomprehensible gibberish. *Been riding the subway since I was six, and I ain't never understood a word they've said the whole time.* There weren't that many people in the station this late at night, and most of them didn't even give Spike or Nikki a second glance.

As she leaped down the last few stairs, she saw that a graffiti-covered uptown D train was pulling out—

—with Spike hanging onto the metal connector sticking out of the last car, still grinning like a fool. He'd gone back to his regular face, and he was waving at her.

All of a sudden, she was back on the 79th Street Boat Basin, forced to watch as Darla sailed away, and unable to do a thing about it.

Not this time.

She ran for the train.

As she passed one man, she heard him say, "*Damn*, bitch, just wait for the next one!"

She leaped for the back of the last car just as it was about to disappear into the tunnel, arms outstretched. Her fingers closed around the dirty, cold metal, and she was able to settle one foot on the metal floor that jutted out from the back of the train. The displaced air from the now fast-moving train whipped through her Afro and blew out her coat behind her like a race-car parachute.

By this time, Spike had already forced the door open, and he kicked her from inside the car. She managed to keep her grip, but almost lost her footing. Quickly regaining it, she kicked back, knocking Spike back into the car, and giving her a minute to steady herself. Spike said something, but she couldn't hear it over the din of the subway train as it clattered down the tracks.

The D ran on the express track, and it wasn't late enough for it to make local stops. That meant it wouldn't be stopping until 125th Street, skipping past seven local stops. She jumped into the last car, the back door sliding shut behind her. Spike came at her with a punch to the stomach, which she took, then grabbed his wrist and flipped him over onto his back.

She took half a second to confirm that there was no one in the car. The last car was usually the emptiest, and this one was no different—though the door to the second-to-last car was shutting, indicating that someone had just gone through it. *Probably ran like hell when Spike came crashing in.*

Spike struggled to get to his feet, but she jumped on top of him, her knees pinning his shoulders and some of the safety pins digging into her own dungarees. She reared back to punch him, but Spike managed to get his feet up and kick her off him, sending her head over heels. She managed to convert it to a flip, doing a quick somersault and getting up to her feet.

When she turned around, Spike was also on his feet, smiling at her. *He's still playing his stupid games, dancing his stupid dance. Time to end this. Time to end him.*

So the next thing they did was something Nikki could only categorize as dancing. Using the poles that ran down the middle of the car, they jumped and kicked, each dodging out of the other's way gracefully, neither one landing a blow—partly because the damn train was wobbling back and forth on the track, making it impossible to plant yourself to get a good kick in.

Then, finally, she was able to nail him in the face with a hook kick, which sent him stumbling over to one of the long benches that lined both sides of the train.

He got up quickly, though, and got in a punch of his own. They started trading blows, and it was Columbus Circle and Central Park all over again, only he was laughing.

Laughing!

That did it for Nikki—she just lost it. Snarling, she deflected one of his punches, whirled around, twisting his right arm in the process, and then held him in place while she hit him with two roundhouse kicks to the stomach with her platforms, then punched him in the face, again sending him sprawling onto the benches. This time, though, she didn't give him a chance to get up, but grabbed him by the back of that *stupid* shirt and slammed his head into the space between the top of the seat and the bottom of the window. Then she walked him across the car and slammed his head right into one of the windows.

It shattered, but the noise was barely audible over the din of the train. In midsummer, the subway trains' windows were all open, which made it nice and loud in the cars, and breaking a window did nothing to quiet things down.

To Nikki's surprise—and revulsion—Spike let out a primal scream while his head was sticking out of the window. Nikki had been hoping that the train was close enough to the sides of the tunnel to rip his head off, but no such luck.

He managed to push his way back into the car and land a few more punches. Nikki's cheeks and jaw burned from the blows, but she was the Slayer, and she could take it.

Then he grabbed her and slammed her into one of the doors, then started punching her in the spleen. It didn't hurt much, though, because of the coat, the latest in a series of reasons why she loved that piece of outerwear. *Not bad for something I found used in the Village for ten bucks.*

She struggled to get her right arm up and then elbowed Spike in the face. As he stumbled back, she grabbed him and started knee-kicking him in the stomach.

He pushed her off, and she stumbled back. Her breaths were starting to get more labored, and the coat suddenly felt incredibly heavy. It had been a long time since a single bloodsucker had given her this kind of trouble. It was starting to become old news.

Hell with this—I'm the Slayer. She reached out, grabbed Spike by the safety pins, and threw him behind her, toward the front of the car. Then she grabbed one of the poles and used it to pivot on a jumping kick that sent the honky bloodsucker reeling, crashing into another pole.

Then he looked at the pole and palm-heeled it. Nikki thought he was crazy, but then the pole broke in two. *Damn, thought them poles was stronger than that.*

Or maybe Spike was the one who was stronger.

He started twirling the pole around like Bruce Lee with one of those big wooden sticks.

That was his first mistake, and Nikki intended to make him pay. He telegraphed that he was going to try to hit her over the head, and sure enough, a second later he tried to hit her over the head. She deflected the blow with ease, and then punched him in the face.

Now she was smiling. *Who's laughing now, turkey?*

And now he was snarling as he came at her again with the pole, moving *incredibly* fast. Before she knew it, sharp pain sliced into her stomach, as the jagged edge of the pole hit her right in the side, unprotected by the coat. Doubling over, she left herself wide open to be hit in the face, the cold metal striking her cheek and sending her to the constantly shifting floor of the subway car.

They raced past the 81st Street stop, which was right under the Museum of Natural History and the Hayden Planetarium. *Robin loves going there—maybe this weekend I'll take him there, see the big blue whale he likes so much....*

Dammit, focus! Forcing her mind back to the present, she started crabwalking backward so she could get her bearings. *Shouldn't have let Spike get me that bad.*

Then he raised the pole up, giving her plenty of time to raise her arms to block it—but this time she grabbed the pole, yanked it away from him, and, for good measure, slammed her platform heels into his groin.

She quickly got to her feet, seeing that Spike looked a little dazed. Pushing past her own fatigue, and trying to throw everything she could into her right arm, she leaped forward with a haymaker that sent Spike sprawling to the floor.

Once again she straddled him, but this time lower so she could keep his legs immobilized. She punched him again and again and again, holding both his arms immobilized with her left hand while she whaled on him.

As they shot past the 86th Street station, the lights went out. *Time to put this sucker to sleep.* She reached into her coat pocket for her stake.

The train lurched.

Nikki lost her balance.

Spike managed to kick up and knock her to the dirt-covered floor. Before she even realized what was happening, *he* was straddling *her*, his hands on her throat. His weight on her stomach and thighs was tremendous, and she couldn't budge; his grip on her throat was like a vise.

She clawed at his arm, but it didn't do any good; she found herself unable to breathe.

For the first time since her grandmother died, Nikki

Wood was scared. She'd been worried lots of times, concerned quite a bit, but since Bernard Crowley had come to her pad and said she was the Slayer, she'd never been scared of anything.

Until now.

Please don't! I have to get home to my son....

Then Spike's grip tightened.

... to my Robin.

Then he grabbed the back of her head.

Take care of him, Crowley.

Then the world ended.

Spike stared down at the corpse of the Slayer.

I did it. I bagged another one.

The first one, that Chinese bird—killing her had been the greatest night of Spike's life. There was never anything quite like the first time, and that particular one was glorious, tasting the Slayer's blood and sharing it with Dru.

But this—this was the greatest *fight* of his life.

Spike had tangled with all sorts of humans, demons, fellow vampires, Slayers, but none of them had given him a rush like this—not least because more than once, Spike had been sure he was going to snuff it, a feeling he'd never gotten in China. Right at the end there, she had him. All she had to do was pull out her stake, and that would've been the end of it. Almost a century of unlife turned to dust.

But then the train lurched, Spike saw his moment, and he took it. Had himself a good day.

The train was lumbering along past the 96th Street

station. Spike got up and stumbled more than walked—now that the fight was over, he was starting to feel every punch and kick the Slayer got in on him, and his muscles and bones ached—over to the red emergency brake handle near the back of the car. He yanked it downward, and the train screeched to a halt. Spike almost fell to the floor from the sudden cessation of motion combined with physical exhaustion after the scrap.

Blood of a Slayer was an aphrodisiac, as Spike well knew from seventy-seven years past, but he couldn't bring himself to drain this one the way he had the Chinese girl. No, Nikki deserved better. She had manipulated him and Dru with a verve that would've impressed Angelus, and then stayed on him to the very last, and didn't beg for mercy or nothing.

Not that he'd share that with anyone. As far as he was concerned, when he was talking about this one with the lads over a pint of blood, he'd say she went down easy and begged for her life. After all, he had a reputation to uphold.

He walked back over to her corpse. Time was running short—someone would be along shortly to check on why the brake was thrown—but he had to do one last thing.

The first Slayer he killed had given him a remembrance: the scar he still carried on his left eyebrow.

This one, who gave him the best fight of his life, she'd leave him something too. Something better.

Kneeling down, he started removing the leather coat.

He stood, wrapped the coat around his back, slid

his arms in, and looked down at himself. *Fits like a bloody glove, it does.*

Then, smiling, he ran toward the back of the car, his new coat billowing behind him. After forcing the back door open again, he ran down the tunnel, back to the 96th Street station. Nobody saw him run over to the local track and then leap up onto the platform, or go downstairs—for reasons Spike neither knew nor cared about, the trains that ran under Central Park West had the uptown and downtown tracks stacked one over the other instead of side by side like in the rest of the city—to wait for a train to take him back to Columbus Circle. *Hope Dru's all right.* He wasn't too concerned—his love could take care of herself, especially with the Slayer out of the picture.

Nothing was really keeping Spike in New York now. He'd seen the Ramones, killed the Slayer, and been reunited with Dru. All was well. Besides, Dru always preferred Europe. Once he found her again, they'd head for the pier and find a boat to stow away on.

A CC train pulled into the station and opened its doors. Spike sauntered in, thinking, *Can't wait to hear what Dru thinks of my new coat....*

Chapter Sixteen

New York City
July 15, 1977
1:35 a.m.

Bernard Crowley was awakened out of a sound sleep by the buzzing of the intercom to the doorman's station at the front door. Noting the time on his alarm clock, he angrily said, "What could it possibly be at this hour?" as he picked up the receiver.

"Sorry, Mr. Crowley, but it's a detective named Landesberg here to see you, along with two uniformed officers."

That burned Bernard's anger to ashes. *What's Arthur doing here?* He couldn't even recall ever giving the detective his address—though he supposed that

Landesberg had his own ways of tracking that down. "Send them up, of course."

He threw on a dressing gown, then opened the door to the guest room to make sure that Robin was sleeping soundly.

Landesberg knocked on the door right after Bernard had put the kettle on and lit up a cigarette.

Opening the door, he saw a hard look on Landesberg's face that he saw only when the detective had witnessed a particularly brutal crime. In deference to the two uniformed officers standing behind him, he went with a more formal greeting: "Detective. Please come in."

Landesberg took two steps into the flat, going in only as far as he had to in order to allow the two officers to also come in and close the door behind him, but not get very deep into the place. "Mr. Crowley, I'm afraid you're going to have to come with us. We need you to identify a body."

The world seemed to spin under Bernard's feet. "Wha—what?"

"There's a body on a subway train near the 103rd Street station just up the street. Afro-American female, no ID, but a card that says in case of an emergency to contact you. I need you to—"

"Yes," Bernard said, his mind in a fog. "I just need—I—Robin, her son, he's—he's asleep, I—I need to—"

Landesberg put a hand on Bernard's shoulder, stopping him from moving toward the hallway. "He shouldn't see this. One of the officers will stay here and keep an eye on the kid." Landesberg turned back to one of the officers, whose nameplate read CLANCY, and nodded. Clancy nodded back.

"Very—very well."

Bernard had no recollection of actually getting dressed, accompanying Landesberg and the other officer downstairs to a waiting police vehicle, then driving the nine blocks up Central Park West to 103rd Street. It was as if Bernard went straight from saying "very well" to materializing at 103rd, getting out of the car, and going under the yellow crime-scene tape that blocked off the intersection.

Nikki is dead. He finally allowed himself to have that thought. *I can't believe it. I thought she'd last longer than this.* While it was true that most Slayers didn't last into their twenties—indeed, most didn't make it to their cruciamenta, and many didn't survive that—Bernard had thought that Nikki would be different.

Why, because you *trained her?* he tartly asked himself as Landesberg led him down the steep staircase to the 103rd Street station. *Are you truly that arrogant?*

The scene that greeted him on the platform reminded him a great deal of the night he'd first met Nikki—dozens of people working for various branches of the NYPD milling about doing whatever duties they had to perform.

In the middle of the platform was a hospital gurney. A sheet had been pulled over the human-body-shaped item on top of it. Bernard suddenly found it hard to breathe, and not just because of the oppressive airlessness that categorized a New York subway platform in midsummer.

Landesberg pulled the sheet down to reveal Nikki's face. Her head was at an impossible angle to the rest of her body.

God, no! Even though he'd been steeling himself for this moment, it was now all Bernard could do to keep from stumbling to the floor. But somehow, he gathered up the remnants of his dignity, stiffened his upper lip, and said, "Her name is Nikki Mavis Wood. She was—a friend. I occasionally babysat for her son, Robin. He's the one you left Officer Clancy with. She lives in a flat over the Gem Theater on 42nd Street."

One of the uniformed officers, who was taking notes, asked, "A *what* over the Gem Theater?"

Shaking his head, Bernard said, "Sorry—apartment."

"Oh, okay."

Bernard answered a few more questions, all basic personal information, then he himself asked, "Where's her coat?"

Frowning, Landesberg asked, "Coat?"

"She—she had a leather coat. She never went outside without it, regardless of the weather."

Landesberg looked over at the uniformed officer, who said, "This is how they found her, Detective."

Finding he could could no longer stand to look at Nikki's body like this, Bernard turned and walked briskly toward the exit, saying, "If that's all, Detective."

Landesberg walked just as briskly to keep pace.

"One more thing, Bernie." It was the first time he'd called him anything other than "Mr. Crowley" since arriving at his flat.

Slowing down his gait so Landesberg could comfortably walk alongside him, but still keep them both moving far away from Nikki's body, Bernard said, "Yes?"

"We got a witness, says two people burst into the back car after it pulled outta 59th. One of them matches your girl. The other one"—he hesitated—"matches the description of that guy who killed those two girls last week."

Bernard stopped walking and closed his eyes. *Spike. Of course. I should've guessed. Nikki said she was going after him and Drusilla tonight.*

For the sake of keeping up appearances, Bernard asked, "Any leads on his whereabouts?"

"Not yet—and if he's what I think he is, we won't get any. And now our best shot at getting the sonofabitch is lying dead on that subway platform."

Tears started to cloud Bernard's vision. He ran his sleeve over his eyes. "I'm afraid so, Arthur."

Landesberg nodded. "I'm sorry, Bernie."

"As am I." Bernard let out a long breath, and then forced his upper lip into stiffness once again. "Now, if you'll excuse me, I must get back to Robin and—and give him the bad news."

By the time Robin cried himself back to sleep, it was almost four in the morning. Bernard felt like he'd been run over. There was no easy way to tell a four-year-old that the mother he adored more than anything in the world was never coming back. Not even when the child was especially bright and aware of what, exactly, his mother did every night. Robin screamed and denied and cried and shouted and insulted.

Then, finally, he fell asleep, leaving Bernard free to make the phone call he'd been dreading having to make from the moment he was first told he was being assigned to a Slayer four years ago.

He dialed the series of numbers that would connect him to Watchers Headquarters in London, eventually being put through to Roger Wyndham-Pryce.

"William the Bloody, eh?" Wyndham-Pryce said. "Yes, I recall him and his paramour at that orphanage in Vienna. Nasty business, that."

Bernard said, "Indeed," remembering that Wyndham-Pryce had been one of the survivors of that little massacre.

"Very well, Bernard, we'll start making the necessary arrangements—see if any of our potentials have activated. In the meantime, you'll need to send the emergency kit back and—"

"I'm afraid," Bernard said quickly, "there is one more piece of business: Robin."

"Who?"

Dear God in heaven, don't any of these blighters read the reports I send them? "Nikki had a four-year-old boy named Robin. He's orphaned now."

"The Slayer had a child? That's most irregular, Bernard, how could you allow such a thing?"

Tightly, Bernard said, "My allowance had very little to do with it, Roger, the child was born before she was called."

"I see." Wyndham-Pryce's tone indicated that he very much didn't, but Bernard let it go. The Watcher continued, "Well, be that as it may, I'm not clear as to the difficulty. I'm sure even as dismal a spot as New York has such things as orphanages."

Horrified, Bernard said, "Are you mad? This child is our responsibility, we can't just—"

"We can and we will, Bernard. Our task is to supervise the Slayers, not clean up the Slayers' mistakes."

"Robin is hardly a 'mistake.' He's a bright young boy whose mother was taken from him."

"He should never have known his mother," Wyndham-Pryce said archly. "You should have insisted she give the child up for adoption the moment you recruited her."

"She would never have stood for that," Bernard said. "I—"

"What she stood for is of no relevance, as you well know. We're fighting a war, after all, and war is no place for children. I have to confess to being disappointed—but not entirely surprised. You were never intended for fieldwork, only observation, so it's no wonder you've failed."

Bernard could have made any number of responses to this. He could have gone the intellectual route and listed Nikki's many accomplishments, from stopping Darla, to keeping New York from being sucked into hell, to defeating Dracula, to destroying the snake demon who called himself Diamondback, to keeping a lid on Reet's activities, to averting more than one apocalypse. He could have gone the childish route and insulted

Roger Wyndham-Pryce's parentage and intellectual capacity. He could have found some middle ground between the two.

Instead, he said, "Very well, I quit," and hung up on the pillock.

Under no circumstances would he sully Nikki's memory by giving up her child to what passed for orphanages in this city. Nor would he return his books, diaries, files, or the emergency kit to England. If Wyndham-Pryce's attitude was representative of the Watchers Council these days, Bernard had no use for them, and he saw no reason to give them aid or comfort. If they asked for any of the material, so be it, but he would not willingly be their lapdog.

He undressed and climbed into bed, beyond exhausted. Tomorrow he would begin the paperwork to formally adopt Robin, and also clean out the apartment at the Gem. *Young Mr. Manguson will no doubt be devastated.* Then perhaps they should move. Bernard didn't fancy the notion of staying in the city—it would serve only to remind him of her.

Perhaps California, he thought as he drifted off to sleep.

Epilogue

Sunnydale, California
January 22, 2002
9:40 p.m.

Buffy Summers had come to the crypt expecting to see Spike alone, so the sight of this other guy who apparently hadn't gotten the memo that Halloween was three months ago kind of surprised her. Ever since being ripped from Heaven by her well-meaning friends, Buffy had been struggling to get through each day. Spike—who had fallen in love with her, a concept that Buffy still hadn't completely wrapped her brain around—had been a source of comfort, of life. *And how sad is it that I go to someone who's dead to feel alive?*

To the guy in the pimp suit, she said, "You are

aware that the seventies ended when the seventies ended, right? I mean, I didn't even know that shade of purple *existed*."

Pimp Boy went all vampy on her and jumped. Buffy dodged the attack pretty easily, considering he may as well have announced it, and then punched him in the face. He ducked a second punch, and then a swipe with her stake.

"Crazy lady said I'd go to pieces for a blond girl in the moonlight," the vampire was muttering. "Son of a *bitch*."

They went at it for a few more seconds, Buffy having no clue what he was talking about and not caring all that much. The fight took them out into the cemetery. Buffy managed to bounce his face off a headstone, and he managed to kick her right into one of the trees.

Spike, meanwhile, was just standing there in the doorway to the crypt.

"The hell's wrong with you, honky? Why you just standin' there? She the *Slayer*, fool!"

Buffy was wondering much the same thing, but not for the reasons Pimp Boy was thinking. He lunged at her with a punch, which she deflected; then she spun around and delivered a spinning hook kick to the back of his neck, knocking him to the grass-covered ground. Pulling out her stake, she went to stab him with it, but he blocked it with his arm and then socked her in the temple, sending her reeling.

She stumbled back a bit, temporarily dizzied from the blow. Turning to Spike, who was standing in the doorway with his arms folded, she said, "Little help here?"

"Wasn't aware you needed it," Spike said with a smile.

Pimp Boy had gotten to his feet now. "Help?" He looked at Spike. "You *helpin'* the Slayer? The hell kinda traitor *are* you?"

"Things change, mate," Spike said.

Buffy smiled. "Except for you, apparently." With that, she stepped one leg behind the other and delivered a side kick to Pimp Boy's stomach, doubling him over. Then she lunged for his chest with her stake.

He was dust a second later.

Pocketing her stake, Buffy turned to Spike, who hadn't moved a single undead muscle. "Did you know this reject from *Shaft*?"

Spike shrugged. "A loose end from a long time ago. Not worth getting worked up over."

"So what was he doing here?"

"What," Spike said defensively, "I'm not allowed to have visitors besides you or your precious Scooby gang? I've got a life, you know."

"And that life includes fun meetings with fashion-free vampires?"

Holding up his arms in a what-do-you-want-from-me gesture, Spike said, "You didn't see me stopping you from dusting the wanker, now, did you?"

"Didn't see you helping me, either." Even as she spoke, Buffy wondered why she was being so defensive. It wasn't as if she needed the help.

"You didn't ask," Spike said, "and I didn't think you needed the help."

Buffy shuddered. *Great, now we're thinking alike.*

Spike went on, "He's just some vampire I knew from the old days, came by to look me up. I was ready to toss him out on his ear when you showed up."

"You said he was a loose end—from what?"

"Just a scrap I got into back in the day."

Again Buffy shuddered. Pimp Boy was dressed in vintage seventies wear. Buffy didn't know all of Spike's history, but she knew what he was doing in 1977, when those fashions were at the height of their inexplicable popularity. *Did that guy help Spike kill that Slayer in New York? Were they planning ways of killing me?*

No, Buffy realized, that was ridiculous. Spike had made his love for Buffy all too clear, to the point where he'd risked everything to save Dawn. Whatever he'd done in the past was in the past.

Kinda like that guy I just dusted.

"I'm sorry," she said in a small voice.

"Well, that's a first," Spike said with a snort. "Nothin' to apologize for, pet. Honestly, you did me a favor. Like I told Leroy before you arrived, only reason he's still alive was 'cause of an oversight on my part. You went and rectified that for me."

Allowing herself a smirk, she said, "In that case, I'd like to claim my reward."

Spike's grin was much wider—and much more greedy. "We aim to please, baby."

She went into the crypt, wondering if making love to Spike—no, screwing Spike, what they were doing had very little to do with love, at least from her point of view—after a fight might make things better.

Somehow, she doubted it, but she went ahead inside anyhow.

He killed a Slayer twice before. I've been dead twice before. He once told me that all Slayers have a death wish, which makes me wonder if that's what keeps me coming back. We have death to share.

However, Buffy voiced none of these thoughts as she grabbed Spike and kissed him with a violence that was borne of both intensity and desire.

Spike closed the crypt door. . . .

Robin Wood was greeted by the young woman behind the desk as he entered the hotel. "Can I help you, sir?"

Putting on his best smile, Robin said, "Yes, I have a reservation, name of Wood."

"Can I see some ID, please, sir?"

Nodding, Robin reached into his back pocket and pulled his California driver's license out of his wallet, as well as his credit card. He'd learned to drive as a teenager in Beverly Hills, where he'd been raised by his adoptive father, Bernard Crowley. Bernard had been a good and kind father, always giving Robin the best of everything.

It wasn't until Bernard was on his deathbed that he told Robin the truth.

The story interrupted regularly by the horrible coughing fits that had characterized his losing battle with lung cancer, Bernard had told the twenty-one-year-old Robin everything about his first four years, about his mother, Nikki, her calling, her duty, and her vicious end at the hands of a vampire. All the martial arts work—Bernard was a third-degree black belt in seido karate, and he had been training Robin for as long as the young man could remember—had finally made sense at that point. Bernard had also told him about the Watchers Council and Bernard's own departure from same. And he had shown Robin the bag that was now the only keepsake he had of his mother.

Suddenly, several shards of memory that had always confused Robin had come into focus. He'd visited New York twice when he was in college and had been struck by parts that seemed eerily familiar despite his not remembering ever visiting the city. Now he realized the truth—he hadn't visited, he'd *lived* there. According to the therapist he'd been seeing for the past few years, the trauma of his mother's death had caused him to repress a great deal of his life prior to the age of four, but working with her had brought most of it back.

The one thing Bernard had refused to share was the name of the vampire who had killed his mother. "You cannot fight him," Bernard had said between coughs. "He is eternal, and you are mortal. I have trained you so you can contribute to the fight against evil, Robin, but revenge is not the way."

Of course, Robin hadn't paid a lick of attention to that advice and had spent most of his twenties trying and failing to track down the vampire who killed his mother. He had also learned quite a bit about Slayers. He had heard about Hemery High School in Los Angeles being the site of an attack, only to discover that the gym had been burned down by a young blond woman—the newest Slayer. Robin had lost track of her for a while, eventually learning of her presence in the nearby suburb of Sunnydale.

But as he had gotten older—and spent his days as a teacher, quickly moving up the ladder to administrator—he had grown wiser, and had soon come to the realization that he was not yet ready for the big fights.

The clerk handed him his credit card and license back. "Are you in town for business or pleasure, Mr. Wood?"

"A job interview, actually," he said. "They're rebuilding the high school, and I've applied to be the new principal."

"Really?" The clerk barked a laugh. "You're a little young, aren't you?"

"To be principal?" he asked with a grin.

"To be that stupid. You know what happened to the last two principals?"

"I heard," Robin said. "That's why I feel good about my chances. I hear I'm the only applicant."

Robin still wasn't sure if he was ready to join the fight that Bernard had trained him for, but he also was unable to pass up the opportunity when word went out that the new Sunnydale High was looking for a principal. Robin had much less experience than other candidates, but other candidates were shying away from the opportunity. The last two principals, after all, had been eaten.

But Robin also knew that Sunnydale High was located right on a Hellmouth. And that meant he'd be right in place to do the best he could to help the fight against evil.

The clerk ran a room key through the card reader, placed it in a piece of cardboard on which she wrote a number, and handed it to Robin. "Your room number is on the envelope, Mr. Wood. Enjoy your stay—and good luck on the interview!"

Smiling, Robin said, "Thanks." Picking up his garment bag and duffel, he walked over to the elevators, anticipating very little sleep. He always suffered insomnia before a job interview, and this one promised much more excitement than most.

Maybe I'll get to help the Slayer out. Wouldn't that make Mama proud?

Historian's Note

The author has endeavored to portray the New York City of 1977—which he remembers fondly from his childhood—as accurately as possible. The "Son of Sam" murders were indeed an ongoing concern, as David Berkowitz had gone a year without being caught, or even identified, as of July 1977, despite the best efforts of the New York Police Department's Operation Omega task force. In addition, the city was in fact in the midst of a brutal fiscal crisis; the NYPD union was in ugly negotiations with the city; Mayor Abe Beame's work-release program was a source of controversy; six people were running against Beame for mayor (the victory eventually went to Ed Koch, who would serve three terms; another of the candidates, Mario Cuomo, would go on to become a beloved governor of the state); the New York Yankees were in the midst of a pennant race (they would go on to win the World Series, the team's first Series victory in fifteen years); the city had almost torn down Grand Central Terminal, though that was averted, not by the Slayer, but by Jackie Kennedy Onassis; Columbus Circle was home to the now long-demolished New York Coliseum; and Times Square was a haven of peep shows, pornography, prositution, and low-rent movie theaters, its Disney-fication still two decades in the future. And, of course, there really was a blackout that commenced at 8:37 p.m. on the 13th of July, one that lasted for twenty-five hours and saw the city gripped by riots, looting, vandalism, and fires.

In some cases, the author has taken liberties for the purposes of the story. For example, while all attempts have been made to capture the spirit of CBGB's in its heyday, there is, in fact, no such band as Apple Corpse, and, while the Ramones were a fixture at CBGB's in the late 1970s, they didn't actually play the club on the weekend of the 8th of July (the punk weekend referred to *did* happen, but it was hosted by the Cramps).

Any other mistakes, flubs, or inaccuracies should be blamed entirely on the author, to whom you can e-mail your raspberries at keith@decandido.net.

Finally, the prologue and epilogue take place shortly prior to the sixth-season *Buffy* episode "Doublemeat Palace."

ABOUT THE AUTHOR

This is **Keith R. A. DeCandido**'s third *Buffy* book: He also helped put together the first edition of *The Watchers Guide* in 1998 and wrote the 1999 novelization *The Xander Years*, Volume 1. As a native New Yorker, having grown up there in the 1970s, he found the character of Nikki Wood appealing from the moment he first saw her and Spike duking it out on the subway in "Fool for Love," and so is thrilled to have been given the chance to write *Blackout*. Keith's other fiction has taken him to the media universes of *Star Trek* (in all its incarnations, plus some new ones), Spider-Man, *Farscape*, *Doctor Who*, *Xena*, Gene Roddenberry's *Andromeda*, *Young Hercules*, and, most recently, novels based on the video games World of Warcraft (Cycle of Hatred) and Starcraft: Ghost (Nova). His original novel *Dragon Precinct* was published in 2004, he novelized the Joss Whedon film *Serenity* in 2005, and he's also edited several anthologies. In what he jokingly refers to as his spare time, Keith plays percussion, practices *kenshikai* karate, and follows his beloved New York Yankees. He still lives in New York City with his girlfriend and two lunatic cats. Find out more insanity at his official website, DeCandido.net.

Buffy the Vampire Slayer™

Into every generation, a Slayer is born...

Before there was Buffy, there were other Slayers—called to protect the world from the undead. Led by their Watchers, they have served as our defense—across the globe and throughout history.

In these collections of short stories written by best-selling authors, travel through time to these other Slayers. From France in the fourteenth century to Iowa in the 1980s, the young women have protected the world. Their stories—and legacies—are unforgettable.

Published by Pocket Books
™ & 2006 Twentieth Century Fox Film Corporation. All Rights Reserved.

You've waited long enough. Find out what happened to Buffy *after* the Hellmouth ate Sunnydale, in this exciting new book!

SUNNYDALE WAS ONLY THE WARM UP
QUEEN of the SLAYERS
NANCY HOLDER

Picking up just after the series finale, Queen of the Slayers *is an exclusive look into the much-missed characters' lives.*

With the closing of the Hellmouth and the "awakening" of hundreds of potential Slayers, Buffy Summers thought she had overturned the Slayer's self-sacrifice and earned herself a much-deserved break of normalcy. But the thrill of victory is short-lived. The Forces of Darkness are not ones to graciously accept defeat.

Willow's magickal distribution of the Slayer essence left girls across the world discovering their latent power. But soon Buffy hears word that a number of the fresh Slayers are being coerced to join an army of Slayers—governed by the mysterious "Queen of the Slayers," an awesome evil determined to claim the intoxicating Slayer essence for herself. The deciding apocalypse is drawing near. Alliances are formed and loyalties betrayed as it comes down to Slayer versus Slayer, leading to an ultimate battle of champions—from Buffy's past and present.

Pocket Books • An imprint of Simon & Schuster • www.simonsays.co.uk
BUFFY THE VAMPIRE SLAYER™ & © 2006 Twentieth Century Fox Film Corporation. All Rights Reserved.